Sarah Tytler

Beauty and the Beast

Vol. 3

Sarah Tytler

Beauty and the Beast
Vol. 3

ISBN/EAN: 9783337048129

Printed in Europe, USA, Canada, Australia, Japan

Cover: Foto ©Andreas Hilbeck / pixelio.de

More available books at **www.hansebooks.com**

BEAUTY AND THE BEAST.

A Novel

By SARAH TYTLER

AUTHOR OF 'THE BRIDE'S PASS,' 'WHAT SHE CAME THROUGH,'
'SAINT MUNGO'S CITY,' ETC.

IN THREE VOLUMES
VOL. III.

London
CHATTO AND WINDUS, PICCADILLY
1884

CONTENTS OF VOL. III.

CHAPTER XXVIII.

REPARATION.

LADY FERMOR gave no token of missing the girl who had been her companion for the last twenty years. The old lady awoke and breakfasted, read the newspapers or got Soames to read them to her, took her stroll on the terrace, ate her luncheon, had her afternoon drive, her nap, her dinner, her evening game of écarté if Major Pollock dropped in, and, failing him, she condescended to a game at cribbage with Soames, retired to bed, and slept apparently without a care on her mind or a feather's weight on her conscience. She had always boasted that, though she was fond of company in her day,

she could suffice for herself, and it looked like
it.   To the few visitors who, remembering
Lady Fermor's position in the county, her
age and isolation, made a point of inquiring
for her, she merely alluded to Iris's absence
without stating its cause or term ; and when
it was Lady Fermor's will to keep her own
counsel, not many people would venture to
dispute the point with her.   Even Lucy,
with the rest of the Acton family and Lady
Thwaite, who were the most surprised and
perplexed at the unexpected, unexplained,
undefined visit somewhere, to somebody,
which Iris was paying, submitted to be kept
for a while in ignorance. Nobody had a
right to intermeddle, nobody suspected even
so formidable an old lady as Lady Fermor
of making away with her grandchild—still
there was something mysterious about the
manner in which Iris Compton had vanished
from her friends' ken, though they easily
learnt that she had left openly, in broad day,
in the Lambford carriage, and taken the
afternoon train to London in the most prosaic
matter-of-fact fashion.   The mystery began
to make itself felt, so that within a fortnight
of the event Lady Fermor's' tranquillity was

disturbed, and she was assailed and called to
account in her own house, which ought to
have been her castle.

Lady Fermor had returned from her afternoon drive, and gone into her drawing-room
for half an hour, when a message was brought
to her from a former friend—a man who had
forgotten the habit of sending in a card almost
as soon as he had acquired it, who had arrived
at the frame of mind when forms and ceremonies were indifferent to him. If he remembered them, good and well; why not
comply with them if they were a matter of
use and wont, and of satisfaction to anybody?
If he forgot them, good and well also; what
did they signify after all to any creature with
a reasonable judgment and a soul to be saved?
Sir William Thwaite could bid a servant tell
Lady Fermor that he wished to see her, and
he forgot himself to such a degree that it
was exactly what he said. He had not the
suavity to add, ' By her ladyship's leave,' or
' If the call is convenient for her,' notwithstanding he had long ceased to be a daily
visitor at Lambford. He had not been there
since the night of Miss Compton's ball. He
had not spoken to Lady Fermor since she

40—2

left him in a rage, in the teeth of a thunder-storm after her last visit to Whitehills. He had been a husband and a widower in the interval.

As the message was delivered to the venerable woman, her sunken eyes gave a warlike flash, and she managed to sit erect after she had snapped out the two words, 'Admit him.' When it came to that, strife, and not peace, was her natural element. In spite of her years, a tough encounter, a rousing contention, a battle of words were more accept-able to her than sluggish rest.

Sir William came to his former haunt, looking too stern to be lightly discomposed and discomfited. He gave a hurried glance round while he was mechanically saying 'Good-morning' to his former ally, and hoping he saw her well ; and the sternness was in-tensified on a face which, when it was not lit up with a smile, had always been more the type of a certain form of comely strength than of physiognomical sunshine and sweetness.

'It is a treat to see you nowadays, Sir William,' said Lady Fermor tentatively, motioning him to a seat beside her.

But he did not sit down, and he did not

answer her, save by telling his errand with brutal straightforwardness. 'Where is Miss Compton, Lady Fermor?'

'Why do you ask?' she parried his question with the utmost coolness and intrepidity, while her eyes twinkled maliciously.

'Because I am determined to know,' he answered after an instant's pause.

'And by what right do you claim to be made acquainted with my grand-daughter's whereabouts?' she repeated her counter-challenge. 'Really, Sir William, you were always an original, and at one time, I believe, I rather liked your originality; but that time is past, and there are limits even to good things.'

Her sarcasm did not ruffle his mood. He had ceased to wince at the prick of such weapons; and he was able to proclaim a right which in his eyes was all-sufficient to authorize his presence and interrogation, 'You were willing to give her and her happiness into my keeping once. Is not that enough to entitle me to ask what has come to her?'

'Very little has come to her, as you say, that I know of,' answered Lady Fermor with an insolent criticism of his English, and with exasperating nonchalance. 'If she had many rejected lovers it would be an awkward precedent to establish that each man might come and bore me with his curiosity to hear the last news of his old flame. But she was not much of a belle, poor thing!—and, to tell the truth, I do not know that she had the glory of dismissing any suitor, save one; therefore, I do not mind saying to you that I know nothing about her.'

'It ain't possible,' he cried hotly; 'she was in your care. Women of your class don't let girls go out into the world on their own hook, to do what they like, without having somebody to look after them. Your notion is, that girls cannot take care of themselves no more than if they were babies.'

'And I dare say we are right,' she interjected briskly.

'And you make and keep them helpless,' he went on without appearing to pay any attention to her, 'till they are too delicate and dainty to stand on their own feet and make their own way. I know she isn't like that, and I haven't such a bad opinion of the world as to think that there are many, either gentle or simple, that would harm her. But it ain't kind or considerate that she should be exposed to what another young lady could not face ; and, though she may not be right-down harmed, she may be frightened and worried. Lady Fermor, I insist on your giving me satisfaction.'

'In my day it was gentlemen who gave each other satisfaction,' said Lady Fermor airily ; 'a good manly custom which, like some other customs not half so bad as they were called, has passed away ; but let them go—they served my time. I assure you, Sir William, I am not accountable for the young lady in whom you are pleased to take so deep an interest. I am sorry not to have it in my power to say she returns it, or would thank you for it,' with a little mocking, palsied bow to her listener. 'She took our relations, hers and mine, into her own hands. According to your definition, she assumed the privilege of the lower orders. She said it was better we should part ; she could not stay any longer with me. I am too old a woman to pretend to fight with disobedient, undutiful girls or boys either, even though they are my grandchildren. She said she would go, and she went—there is the long and the short of it.'

'Before it came to that, my lady, you had something to answer for,' said Sir William, gulping down what was sticking in his throat.

'Now, don't you think this is getting tiresome?' suggested Lady Fermor. 'I have told you the truth, which, whatever you may believe, you have no earthly call to swagger here and demand from me. May I beg you to spare me your reflections on it, and to cut short your visit? Don't you see, man, I have come in from a drive, and am tired?'

'I cannot help it,' he protested, but in the middle of the rudeness he pushed a foot-stool under her feet, and caught up a cushion to place at her back. Remembering former services of the same kind, rendered under different circumstances and highly valued then, the wicked old face twitched and softened a little, though it relapsed the next moment into its malice and hardness.

'You don't mean to say you let her go like that?' he persisted, still standing like an avenging giant before a hard-hearted witch. 'You never asked her where she was to turn to ? You are not acquainted with any friend she might seek ?'

'No,' she had the coarseness and cruelty to answer him; 'it is not always advisable to ask too many questions. We women are not often without friends at Iris's age ; and we don't always care to publish the road we mean to follow. It is a pleasant enough road at starting, whatever you men may make of it in the end.'

'It is a shameful lie !' he said, speaking his mind without the slightest reservation, while his fresh-coloured face darkened to a dusky red, and the veins on his forehead, within the curves of chestnut hair, stood out knotted like whipcord. 'By George, if you were a man, though you were a prince, I would not stand to hear it. You are an old woman and my lady; but I say you have spoken an infamous slander against your own flesh and blood, as much above you as heaven is above earth. Where is your natural womanly feeling, your mother's heart, Lady Fermor ? I was a fool to come near you, unless to speak a bit of my mind, and denounce you in the place where you be-fooled me.'

Something in his air and attitude smote the rock of her nature on which his words had struck in vain. She shrank and cowered a little, and collapsed into the feebleness of her years.

'Don't,' she implored, 'don't you curse me ; you are like—like a friend I had once. Never mind who it was. I saw the likeness the first day we met, and took a fancy for you, and did my best to serve you. I don't deserve this treatment from you, Thwaite, but I am ready to give you satisfaction—all the satisfaction I can. That goose of a girl you think so much of, though she don't care a straw for you, and she ain't worth your trouble—well, let that be—she never told me where she was going, and I am not bound to know ; but she is no more fit to carry out a plot than that Spanish ass, Don Quixote. She behaved like a simpleton, as you may be sure. Her baggage was addressed to the care of a sister of a canting mischief-making governess the child once had, and her ticket was taken to London. She had money for her board for three months. I can give you the address if you care to have it, though I don't see what good it will do

you now. Sir William, will you go and leave
me alone in peace, and don't come back to
haunt me in another person's guise on my
dying bed.'

'No, I want to do something better than
that,' he said, half with lingering fury, half
in gruff relenting and concession to their old
friendly relations. 'You say you took a
fancy for me, and meant well by me. I am
willing to believe you, though it was a fancy
which played me strange tricks, and went
far to my undoing. I was not ungrateful,
whatever you may think. I take it you have
not so many true friends to call your own at
the close of your long life that you should
shake off this one and that one—your grand-
daughter, as good as gold, or even a rough,
little-worth fellow like me. Why in the
name of goodness should you not go after
Miss Compton, find her, and be a loving
grandmother to her, as I am sure she would
be a loving child to you, if you would let
her ?'

'Because it ain't in me, Thwaite,' replied
her ladyship, with returning coolness and
candour. 'You must be a bad reader of
character, if you cannot decipher that.

" Loving grandmother," indeed ! Bah ! I
leave that to your tame old body who has
kissed her faithless tyrant's feet, and run
after her prodigal sons and fast daughters,
until in the evening of her days she is content to sit chirping and snivelling over her
mischievous brats of grandchildren.'

He was not to be diverted from his aim.

' You say Miss Compton has the payment
of her board, among people you disapprove
of, for a month or two. What is she to do
then ?   What is she to think now as to what
is to become of her afterwards ? Will you
let her feel herself forsaken by man ?—not by
God.   You cannot touch her there.' He
broke off in a low tone with a mixture of
reverence and tenderness — the true chival-
rous devotion, very different from any species
of love poor Lady Fermor had ever given or
taken, shining in his blue eyes. ' You do
not intend Lord Fermor's grand-daughter to
beg her board from strangers, or to hire herself out for a wage, do you ? though she
might count it no dishonour to make service
honourable by discharging it.'

' She has chosen her course, and she must
abide by it, ay, and eat the fruit of her

folly,' argued the old woman, before she
changed her cue, and suddenly made a concession. 'If I do anything more for Iris
Compton, it will be as a favour to you,
Thwaite. The hussy—or the angel, if you
prefer it—shall owe my forgiveness to you.
That will be something for her pride to
swallow, though I fear you have lost the
spirit to cast it in her teeth.'

Powerful as Sir William's championship
had been, this was not exactly true. It was
a fact that Lady Fermor, like most women
of strong passions, had possessed little
natural affection. The passions had burnt
themselves out, but in their ashes there were
few elements for the growth of the domestic
charities. Still, there were bounds to her
callousness and vindictiveness. Stoically as
she had borne herself, it was impossible for
her not to have experienced twinges of compunction for the grand-daughter of Lord
Fermor, the wrinkled, tottering woman's
lover in the days of her prime, who had
wedded her dishonour, and crowned her
with all the gifts of fortune he could bestow
to the last. Lady Fermor had driven this
girl, as Sir William had put it, from the

dignity and ease of Lambford, to beg her
bread or to hire herself out for a wage. In
the end the old woman might not be unwilling, for more reasons than one, to yield
to his advocacy, giving it all the credit in
order to save her own consistency; while
underneath the veil she appeased her grizzly
ghost of a conscience, and retained the rags
of reputation she had recovered in the
world.

'Thanks,' he said shortly; and then,
fearing to displease her, and turn her from
her cautious admission, he forced himself to
protest, 'I'll stand no end indebted to you
if you do this kindness to yourself and Miss
Compton at my bidding. But what you
mean to do, you ought to set about quickly.'
He betrayed his doubt and anxiety in his
last hesitating words.

'You are in a great hurry, Thwaite,' observed Lady Fermor sarcastically. 'I suppose you see I have my bonnet on my
head, and you think I shall be ready to stir
my old bones and rise and run after a flighty
fool of twenty or thereabouts. Much obliged
for your consideration for my age and infirmities. You had better order the carriage

back at once, and ride on before, and get a
ticket for London, and let me start napless
and dinnerless. I should arrive dizzy and
starving before midnight. I dare say I
might knock about for a bed, or if I found
my way to Fitzroy Square, perhaps my good
grand-daughter would have the common
humanity to lend me hers for what remained
of the night.'

'You are talking nonsense,' he said
bluntly, staring at her, 'but you will go up
to London, and seek out Miss Compton—
won't you?'

'I may, if you will be my escort. I have
never been accustomed to travel without a
squire,' she said with a kind of ghastly
coquetry. 'When I was younger, a good
deal younger, I used to have half-a-dozen
sparks and beaux at my disposal. As it is,
I am not so strong and nimble as Iris
Compton. By-the-bye, I'm not at all sure
that she will give in, and consent to put
herself under my wing again. Disobedience
is a virulent as well as a common complaint
nowadays. I shall need all the foreign support I can get. Yours may not be very
available in this case, but it is better than

none. To be sure, my young lady may have
eaten her leek and changed her mind, while
another person has had time and reason
enough to alter his opinion.   I shan't blame
him, though I am reduced to wonder whether
he has attacked me out of a spirit of contradiction and devilry, or from mere mawkish
magnanimity, pity, and such-like stuff.'

She looked at him sharply.   He returned
her glance coldly, and dismissed her wonder
with a formal 'Good-afternoon, Lady Fermor.   I shall see you to London if you like,
at whatever time you fix upon,' as he left
her.

That night Bill Rogers was considerably
impressed by finding himself put in authority
at Whitehills, while his master held himself
in readiness to start any day for London.

CHAPTER XXIX.

YOUTH STRIVES.

Iris had reached London in safety; she had found Mrs. Haigh, a fat, florid, over-dressed woman, not inhospitable, not un-friendly—far from it. But Iris had not found another Miss Burrage—it would have been unreasonable to expect it in the matron who was in an extraordinary flutter of mingled pride and alarm at having Lord and Lady Fermor's grand-daughter again under Mrs. Haigh's roof. Iris's presence lent a glorious distinction to the upper middle-class boarding-house, but it might be draw-ing down upon the hostess the wrath of 'the combined aristocracy'—and the combined aristocracy must be an awful power indeed—because of Mrs. Haigh's aiding and abetting insubordination in their ranks and desertion from their leaders.

Iris had said honestly : ' I am sorry to say grandmamma and I have not been happy together lately, Mrs. Haigh. Perhaps my dear old friend, Miss Burrage, may have said something long ago, which will help you to understand matters. I don't mean that I am not to blame. No doubt I have failed in tact and patience, and a thousand things, but the painful fact remains that we have not got on well together. Now I have left Lambford with Lady Fermor's knowledge, and come up to town to ask if you will take me in, till I see what is to become of me.'

Of course Mrs. Haigh would take Iris in. What mistress of a boarding establishment, unless she were a very exceptional person, would refuse to receive a peer's grand-daughter, looking as Iris looked, wearing the dress she wore, even if there had not been the old family connection of which Mrs. Haigh had boasted for the last fifteen years ?

Mrs. Haigh was soon satisfied that Iris, though she as good as announced that she had quarrelled with her grandmother, was neither impecunious in the meantime, nor possessed by any romantic delusion of throwing herself on the devotion of ancient allies, and living on air, her dignity, and their worshipping commiseration. When this important little item was agreeably settled to Mrs. Haigh's practical mind, she had nothing to disturb her but the apprehension of Lady Fermor's displeasure, and that vague horror of the wrath of the combined aristocracy which was not without its breathless charm, like the coveted terror produced by an exciting ghost story. Certainly Mrs. Haigh was aware that Lady Fermor had been a very formidable, unmanageable person, though she ought by this time to be in her dotage. But whether doting or not, surely she would rather have her grand-daughter in Fitzroy Square, with highly respectable people of whom her ladyship knew something, than wandering through the world without chaperon or companion—a deplorably compromising style which was not to be 'thought of for a moment, which Mrs. Haigh would never have listened to where her own daughter Juju was concerned. Lady Fermor ought rather to feel relieved and grateful when she heard Mrs. Haigh's name mentioned in the light of a temporary guardian for Miss Compton.

Having persuaded herself of this qualifica-
tion to Lady Fermor's displeasure, Mrs. Haigh
was at liberty to rejoice in the acquisition to
her circle, even though her reason whispered
it could not be permanent.   Its reflected *éclat*
might long survive its actual existence, and
while it lasted the mistress of the house could
load Iris with overpowering attentions.   She
—Mrs. Haigh—could insist on Miss Compton's taking precedence of the other lady-
lodgers, who, to do them justice, evinced no
radical or communistic principles on this
point, but were more than willing to give
way to Iris if she would but shed upon them
a share of the light of her aristocratic countenance.

Her false position hurt Iris, though she did
not attribute it wholly to snobbishness and
vulgarity.   She knew there was a subtle
attraction in rank, and though she both
laughed and winced at the application of the
attraction to herself, in her present circumstances, she was honest enough to own that
she too would have deferred to a duchess,
especially if she had been of the blood royal,
and that a similar homage might only be
different in degree.   But a duchess without

a home, a duchess who was anxiously medi-
tating how she might earn her bread, had
better not have the trappings of her original
estate brandished before her; she ought to
keep them in the background as much as
possible, and take up her position on a common
level.

Iris was vexed that Mrs. Haigh would
constantly speak of her and to her as 'Lady
Fermor's grand-daughter.' The excellent
woman would even betray at once her ignorance and vanity, by bestowing on Iris a
handle to her name to which she was not
entitled. Mrs. Haigh always called Iris the
Honourable Miss Compton, and considered it
foolish modesty and shyness—perhaps a little
hauteur in disguise—when the girl first
hinted, and then said plainly, that neither
the Herald's Office nor Debrett would
authorize the use of such a privilege.

Iris was still more wounded when she had
reason to suspect that Mrs. Haigh, in her
incessant reference to Lambford and Lady
Fermor, did not refrain from imparting in
mysterious whispers, to chosen members of
her circle, the scandals with which [the name
had been associated, or else, by nods and

shrugs and hinted innuendoes, refreshed her
ladies' and gentlemen's memories on the subject. She was irreproachable in her own
morals, yet she seemed to take a warped
pride in what she was pleased to view as
aristocratic iniquities.

These ladies and gentlemen were perfectly respectable, better-class *pensionnaires*.
Though the ladies had the priority by courteous phrase, the gentlemen were really the
ruling power in the establishment, as they
still are in the world. Whether married or
single, from the bachelor confidential clerk in
a tremendously great banking establishment,
to the retired clergyman and half-pay officers,
they all paid board in full; and as they were
the members of the establishment who were
the most out of the house at their offices and
clubs during the day, the gentlemen were
supposed to give the least trouble to their
hostess.

But the supposition was in a great measure
a delusion. It was for the gentlemen's appetite and tastes that Mrs. Haigh catered most
sedulously; it was the gentlemen's evening
rubber that she guarded from interruption
most carefully. Wives sometimes saved her

the trouble of ascertaining their husbands' inclinations, and providing for the men's recreations, by proving beyond mistake that the women were the better horses in the matrimonial traces—were it only in the confident assertion of their inclinations and of their amusements as the first to be considered by their submissive husbands, and, after them, by the rest of creation. But in that case there was merely a reversal of relations, and these potent wives filled their husbands' shoes and represented the men in the boarding-house. The other women—especially the single women—did not fare the better for the exceptions to the supremacy of the men, and to the natural deference shown them by the women.

Some of the spinsters were ladies in reduced circumstances, and paid Mrs. Haigh a smaller board for rooms nearer the sky, and for inferior attendance generally, with which, in strict justice and logic, these half-indigent gentlewomen ought to have been contented. But the fact was they employed a considerable amount of their time either in jealous inspection of the better position of their neighbours, and muttered grumbling over

their own wants, or in high-faluting, ostentatious professions of indifference to circumstances, or else in judicious, assiduous attentions to their better-off companions—attentions which had their reward.

To the single ladies, more than all the
other inhabitants of the house, Iris's advent
was a windfall. For once the spinsters felt
equal to the men and to the married women,
who, by force of character or temper, were as
good as the men, or who merely held on by
the skirts of their individual partners. The
other maidens, however ancient, shared in
the fuss made about a girl, in the special
consideration lavished on her—with much of
which she would willingly have dispensed—
as if it had been a tribute to the whole body
of unprotected females.

In return for the homage paid to her—or
rather to Lady Fermor's grand-daughter—
Iris made figuratively a series of courteous
bows, and sought to possess her soul in
patience like a princess on a royal progress.
But, although in her faith, hope, and charity—
which, after all the sneers liberally launched
at these graces and their Christian origin, are
as trustworthy touchstones as any that have

yet been found for use in the motley crowd of life—Iris had no doubt that there was more than sufficient to respect, like, and inspire interest in her fellow-boarders, if one only knew them better, and held the clue to the true life beneath the conventional; still, looking only on the surface, she did not find material which attracted her particularly in any of the members of the large family under Mrs. Haigh's roof.

Iris was not absorbed, to the withdrawal of her mind from her personal affairs, in the rich, stiffened, silent, white-haired clerk of so great a banking-house, that even its first clerk was surrounded by a nimbus of golden influence and responsibility.

She did not yield to the lively fascinations of Captain Boscawen, who knew all the gossip of the best society, and being affable, gallant, and chatty, was a favourite with most of the ladies. She was not even greatly touched by the Rev. Edward Calcott, a younger man than the first two heroes. He had been forced to retire from his vicar's charge on account of an abiding relaxed throat and weak chest, and was, therefore, as a clergyman and a confirmed invalid, invested

with the double attributes of a spiritual
director and an object of tender sympathy to
every soft heart.   Iris was sorry for him,
but her heart was not so soft in this quarter
as to prevent her perceiving that he was both
self-conscious and self-indulgent; so she left
the nursing of him to his wife, and kept her
spiritual concerns out of his reach.

Iris was not more won by the ladies—from
bluff Mrs. Judge Penfold, who, arguing from
her title, had appropriated her husband's
office as well as the reins of his phaeton—
wherever the colonial law authority, himself,
bridled and saddled, was driven metaphori-
cally—down to little Mrs. Rugely.

The last was an inconsolable pretty young
widow, who, to the envy of the remaining
men, sat bereft at the Rev. Edward's feet ;
yet she was able to take the deepest interest
in the exact fit of her widow's gown and the
becoming shape of her bonnet, and pensively
asked her friends' advice whether scarlet
flowers were not admissible after the first
stage of mourning was past ?   Her lost love
had always liked her with scarlet, and entire
black was really too trying for a brunette
complexion.

Iris had received a blow in finding Mrs. Haigh so unlike Miss Burrage, and the blow was not softened, neither was the likeness increased, on the only occasion when the girl spoke of her best friend to that friend's sister.

Mrs. Haigh twinkled away a facile tear, indeed, and expressed her thankfulness for having had her dear Emily in Mrs. Haigh's house, to be waited upon by her during the good soul's last illness.

' It was a great privilege, Miss Compton ; you who knew her, and who, I may say, was her pet pupil, can guess how uncomplaining, considerate, even cheerful, she was to the very last.'

But Mrs. Haigh was honest in her thick-skinnedness, and absence of deep or delicate or abiding feelings. She added, innocently enough, in the next breath :

' It was a mercy the illness was short, for it saved the dear saint a great deal of suffer-ing ; and to have had her lying long here, or even lingering on, neither ill nor well, unfit for duty, without a sufficient provision for her needs, a burden to herself and others—as, between ourselves, I think Mr. Calcott is sometimes, when he murmurs so at his chimney smoking, and objects to the piano being played after certain hours—would have been more than I could have undertaken, with my husband and children and the care of a boarding-house on my hands. When one comes to think of it all,' reflected Mrs. Haigh with a species of complacency, ' darling Emily was not suited for this world. She was an excellent creature, but she was painfully plain from a girl. She had ability and accomplishments ; but she had no manners that I could see—though, of course, we know she lived in the best society—no " go " or dash. She could not relish what most people enjoy. To dress what I call well became a bore to her. She was not fond of shopping or calling or dining out, and hardly cared for a box or a stall at the opera or the theatre, unless the play or the opera, as well as the singers and actors, chanced to be exceptional. She pottered about more than she was able among humdrum, fallen-down people she had known long ago, or sick or poor people. She had a regard for out-of-the-way churches and eccentric clergymen that few people save herself had heard of or cared for. Put her down with a book she liked and her work, and the world held little more attraction for her. No, poor dear Emily was not a woman for this world. She was a woman to be over-looked and slighted—which she did not mind, for she had rather a lack of spirit and proper pride. She was apt to be smiled at, for she had her little peculiarities, dear soul! though she was my sister—and jostled against and trampled upon, as the world goes. I trust she is far better off where she has gone, poor love!'

'She was a woman of whom the world was not worthy, Mrs. Haigh,' said Iris hotly.

To compare Miss Burrage to Mr. Calcott! To have been capable of thinking of her as a possible burden, and so finding her premature death in one light a boon, instead of wrestling with God that the loved presence might be spared for a season, and yearning to keep it here so long as life lingered in the feeble frame, and sense and love on the peace-ful, wasted brow and lips! There might have been a kind of selfishness in the struggle, and the anguish, and the contest for another with the last foe, in the dumb

despair and hopeless rebellion, which only
God could change into resignation; but it
was the involuntary, inevitable protest against
the separation which, though it be but for a
time, is, next to sin, the sting of death and
the mortal terror and great tribulation of
true love.

What would not Iris have given to have
seen her old friend's dear face again, though
it had come but in a vision of the night—to
have heard her wise, gentle counsel, though
it had been only in a dream !

Iris was not disappointed in Mr. Haigh as
she was in Mrs. Haigh. He was only Miss
Burrage's brother-in-law, by Mrs. Haigh's
election, not a member of Miss Burrage's
family, of the same father and mother, and
of kindred blood. Besides, Iris had retained
a dim recollection of him—more correct in
all respects than her early vision of his wife
as a lively, handsome young matron, who had
petted her and been very affectionate to Miss
Burrage. Mrs. Haigh was still animated
and motherly in hostess fashion, good-looking
in a full-blown style, effusive in caressing
terms and in hugs where she was intimate

enough and could take the liberty to bestow them.

But unfortunately, **Iris** had learnt to know that very little lay behind these signs save what, after all, they might have been fairly taken to indicate by more experienced persons—a creditable, energetic effort to obtain for herself and her family that independence and comfort which Mr. Haigh alone could not ensure to them, natural affection for her offspring, and a considerable fund of careless good-humour.

Mr. Haigh was the cipher that **Iris** had always remembered him. He sat at the foot of the table and did the principal carving. He kept the gentlemen company when the ladies had retired. He was safe for a partner at whist, unless somebody else wished to make up the party. He could serve as a tolerable second when the boarders happened to be musical and a second was in request. He dabbled a little in art, so as to have the *entrée* to a few studios, and afford the benefit of his opinion to any amateur artist in the house. He had the same intangible connection with the theatres and opera-houses, so that he could always procure tickets, boxes

and stalls, and predict what a play would
turn out, when the mass of the public was
helpless and voiceless.   Mr. Haigh had been
educated abroad, and possessed an additional
advantage, of which he was rather vain.   He
was tolerably conversant with several Euro-
pean languages.   He could serve on a pinch
as an amateur courier by anticipation to inexperienced projectors of continental tours.

To all these positive advantages, he added
the strong negative recommendation that he
was without expensive vices.   He might be
said to earn his pocket-money, with the leisure
from all employment save that of obliging
and entertaining his boarders—a duty to
which he was rather partial.

In any other position, Mr. Haigh might
have been a purely ornamental member of
society ; but as the spouse of a lady who kept
an upper-class boarding-house, he was almost
the right man in the right place—while Iris
had never imagined she would get anything
more than a host's gentlemanlike notice from
Mr. Haigh.

But Mrs. Haigh had children, who were
also Miss Burrage's nephews and nieces.
They were all at school save one, Juliana,

or Ju-ju, the eldest daughter, a girl of nine-
teen, to whom Iris turned eagerly. But,
alas! Ju-ju was more like her well-bred
lymphatic father than her mother—far less
her aunt. Ju-ju's chief end in life seemed
to be to comply with all the obligations of the
most finished young ladyhood in the fashion
of the day, under such difficulties as limited
means and the necessity for the family's keeping boarders implied. Ju-ju took her stand
on her father and mother's claims to gentility
as educated people, the children of a clergyman of the Church of England on the one
hand, and a captain in the army on the other.
She ignored the items that Mrs. Haigh had
been a governess like her sister, and that
Mr. Haigh had failed in succession as a barrister, an operatic singer, an artist, and a play-
wright. Ju-ju was inclined to make out that
her father and mother kept a boarding-house
for their private pleasure. She did nothing
save sit embroidering the artistic, elaborate
embroidery of the hour, and attend to her
toilet in the minutest details of the rosette
on her French shoe, and the extra button on
her profusely buttoned glove.

She was neither pretty nor plain, though

she had a good figure, and felt the more persuaded on that account that dress was of the first consequence to her. She had her own visiting set picked out from the sets of various boarders who had taken her into company with them. Mrs. Rugely and Mrs. Judge Penfold usually chaperoned her instead of her busy mother.

Iris Compton contemplated Ju-ju from a puzzled mental and moral distance, with the puzzle deepened by the fact that the girl was Miss Burrage's niece. How could personal enjoyment and the idlest trifles engross her wholly? What was she thinking of when she sat calmly applying herself for so many hours to this costly fancy-work, while her mother, behind backs, was really cumbered with the care of her servants, the burden of housekeeping for a large, disconnected, troublesome family, the worry of account-books which frequently refused to 'square'? And what became of all the splendid and delicate embroidery, of which only a few finished specimens appeared in the shape of table-covers and cushions in the drawing-room? Did Ju-ju simply work it to train and gratify her hand and eye, and then wantonly destroy it, or did she bestow it as presents on all her absent friends ?

Iris found out the enigma at the same time that she hit upon a little opening for her own unprovided-for future, which was beginning to weigh heavily upon her mind.

In vain had Iris asked Mrs. Haigh's advice about what she ought to do to earn a little money. Mrs. Haigh was convinced that Iris's illustrious relations would not permit such an indignity. Miss Compton would only require to hint to them that her coffers were becoming empty, to have them filled again to overflowing.

Mrs. Haigh was not sure but that the law could compel a suitable provision, for she had read of peers' heirs who went to law to drag a maintenance from their stingy fathers, and she did not see why peeress's heiresses might not do the same. If it were not so, an aristocrat-adoring country would be enchanted to support Iris without compulsion.

In vain Iris frankly approached the subject with some of the other ladies—counting on them as a sort of informal women's friendly society. She was always stopped by their smiling and pooh-poohing her. They would not have their peer's grand-daughter pulled down from her pedestal, or else they regarded her prospects with regard to working for her bread as so hopeless, that they preferred not to discuss them with her. In fact they told her it was lowering herself by hinting at such an alternative, almost as much as if she were to propose to borrow money from them.

At the same time Iris found to her dismay that life in a Fitzroy Square boarding-house, apart from the board, was a great deal dearer than life at Lambford. Everybody over-dressed, punctiliously, with studied variety, for dinner. In the light of Mrs. Judge Pen-fold's brocade and diamonds the one day and velvet and pearls the next; Mrs. Rugely's diaphanous black and jet, or gold; and Ju-ju Haigh's earnestly thought out, subtle har-monies in strange, wonderful stuffs and tints from art-shops, her beads from Venice, her bangles from India, her amber and filigree-work from Damascus—all bought in London town, for Ju-ju had been no traveller—Iris was more than outshone. In such a white India muslin, with turquoise ornaments, as had dazzled Sir William Thwaite, or in such a blue silk, festooned with hops, as would have been

voted decidedly 'swellish' by the Hollises at
Thornbrake, and pronounced perfectly exquisite by the Actons at the Rectory, she
knew she looked shabbily, stalely monotonous
in costume. She was like the poorest of the
poor lady-boarders in their black silks or
black grenadines, with a couple of boddices
to wear alternately, and further changes
wrought in the owners' imaginations by one
set of ribands and flowers in the room of
another. Mrs. Haigh, while she overlooked
the delinquencies of the gentle paupers, would
glance reproachfully at Iris. The Honourable
Miss Compton might do many things as she
chose, but she ought to comply with the rules
of the house in dressing according to her
rank.

The days had long gone by since ladies felt
well equipped with a couple of evening dresses,
by which they were as well known as by their
features and complexions—the last were tolerably permanent in the early ages. The only
question then was, as in the case of Petrarch's
Laura, whether the fair one should appear in
her green with violets, or in her purple with
grey feathers.

Iris had the impression that she was play-

ing at being a grand demoiselle in an effemi-
nate, luxurious, extravagant court. She tried
to resist, but she was a young woman without
a home, and had to yield something to what
Mrs. Haigh called ' the rules of the house.'
She was forced, like the poor ladies, since she
had not the endless resources of Ju-ju, to
waste a great deal of time in contriving small
transparent devices for her dress to pass mus-
ter among the elaborate shifting toilets of the
company.

It was on an errand to procure some not
too costly, gauzy transformation, that Iris,
who had from the first claimed the liberty of
walking out by herself without becoming a
mutual drag and fetter either on Mrs. Haigh
or Ju-ju, visited such a monster shop of all
wares as is a remarkable feature of the London of to-day. It was a little of an enter-
prise even for so fearless a girl as Iris to
enter one of the many doors, fall into a stream
of purchasers, pass down the streets of
counters, and be bewildered by the different
departments of the business, in story after
story of the blocks of buildings. She could
imagine herself in a huge prosaic set of
bazaars, where the babel of tongues all pur-

ported to be one language, and the trans-
mission of her insignificant self from point
to point, by detachments of the army of men
in clergymen and butler-like black coats and
white-chokers, or by phalanxes of girls in
endless black gowns and frizzled hair—professed to be means to an end.

Iris felt so small and so swallowed up,
that she uttered a little cry of pleasure when
she discovered Ju-ju Haigh at a counter on
which the exquisite materials for some of her
embroidery were displayed.

Ju-ju could not be said to return the compliment by sharing in the gratification. She
reddened, and had a constrained air, while
the girls exchanged half-a-dozen words. Iris
would have passed on, but the crush of
buyers and sellers was great here, and she
could not advance many steps before one of
the elder shopwomen, or ladies of the establishment as they prefer to be called, came
to Miss Haigh and delivered a courteous
verbal message:

' If the piece be done by next week, madam' (old-fashioned modes of address have
acquired fresh life and new associations in
connection with London shops), ' Mrs. Cree

says it will be in time enough for the Coun-
tess.'

Ju-ju met Iris's surprised eyes, and immediately turned aside, crimsoning from brow
to throat, through the pearl-powder which
she and young Mrs. Rugely and elderly Mrs.
Judge Penfold and Mrs. Haigh, and poor
Miss Swan, the poorest of the poor ladies,
did not hesitate to use, though they stopped
short as yet of rouge.

But Ju-ju showed no further inclination to
be left alone ; on the contrary, she hurried
over her business, offered to join Iris and
help her, with Ju-ju's valuable aid, in a pur-
chase, and seemed even anxiously desirous of
bearing Miss Compton company in her walk
home.

The motive was soon explained. Whenever
the girls got into the quieter streets, Ju-ju
spoke with almost painful earnestness :

'You have found me out, Miss Compton,
without being able to help it. I embroider
at home, for Mr. Blackburn's art department.
I dare say you have observed that I work
rather closely, though embroidery is a pleasure
to me also. Other people in the house have
noticed it, though of course nobody asks any

questions. My mother can only afford me a small allowance. I could not dress and go out like other girls, if I had not an additional income. I assure you, many girls design or embroider on private commissions, which are the best, as they are for friends ; or for the art-schools, where the girls have been taught ; or for art departments in some of the great shops, and nobody outside is any wiser. The rage for art-work is such a boon to people who would not think of working in any other fashion. Art-work can be done by any lady, without loss of caste, and if you will believe me, many ladies do it for pay who are in no want of money, as I am sorry to say I am. Some of these are connected with the nobility, as you are, and, for the most part, they do not care though it is known they embroider for money. They laugh and boast of it, and are as proud of their earnings as if they were sums gained at Monte Carlo, or the payment of wagers, or the prices of books or pictures which the girls had written or painted. I have heard of girls who have had the sovereigns that have been worked for pierced so that the workers might dangle and display them at their watch-chains, like so

many charms.   But it is a different thing
when working is a necessity.   I don't think
I should work if I had a good allowance or
a rich father,' admitted Ju-ju; 'and I believe,
in my case, it is certainly much better to say
nothing about it.   So, Miss Compton, I shall
be very much obliged to you if you will not
mention what has come to your knowledge
to-day—not even to my mother, though I
need not say she is aware of my arrangement
and has given her full consent to it.'

This was a revelation to Iris, but she did
not stop to enquire if the game were worth
the candle.   She did not weigh against each
other the false pride of girls like Ju-ju Haigh,
who eked out their means and supplied themselves with foolish extravagances by labouring
in strict secrecy for tinsel—not bread; and
the childish vanity of the wealthy aristocratic
girls who vaunted their uncalled-for achievements in the shape of working, at will, for a
few sovereigns, twice the number of which
the workwomen wasted every day they lived.
It just crossed Iris's mind that there was a
performance resembling this on the part of
the ladies of the French *noblesse*, before the
great revolution, when dainty fingers osten-

tatiously unravelled gold thread in lace
which had decorated coats of husbands or
brothers or sons, and sold it as bullion.
But she drew no inference from the comparison.

Iris did not even speculate how it comes
that to work at art designs and marvels of
embroidery, which after all, beautiful as they
may be, are superfluities, can be more honourable than to work at the homeliest useful
work, which is of still greater necessity to
the welfare of the world than the coin with
which the primitive toil is remunerated ; she
only thought that she too could do this art-
work, while she might not be fit for any
other.

She had delighted as a simple matter of
taste, when she was a girl at ease, in the
revival of art embroidery. She had practised
it with enthusiasm, and had attained some
local eminence by her performances. She
had watched Ju-ju's achievements with intelligent admiration, and been able to offer
her available suggestions and help sometimes.
Now Iris ventured to propose, a little breath-
lessly in her excitement :

'Could I do anything for Blackburn's ?

Would they care to employ me ? I should
be glad—thankful, if they would try me. I
need not say I would do my best to give
them satisfaction.'

Ju-ju received the proposal more graciously
and encouragingly than her mother and the
other ladies had met Iris's candid statements
of the obligation on her to find work and
wages. Ju-ju, confident in her own skill and
experience, feared no competition in her
special province, while, on the other hand,
she was inclined to clutch at another example
and to prove that lady-like girls, even girls
connected with the nobility, freely adopted
her calling. The work had something refined
and picturesque in it, after all, recalling old
queens and chatelains with their noble
maidens and bower-women, the Bayeux
tapestry and other less ambitious but still
remarkable performances.

Ju-ju readily undertook to communicate
with Blackburn, and exhibit some specimens
of Iris's capability as a nineteenth-century
Arachnë. Mrs. Haigh shook her head, and
was troubled by the anomaly ; but Ju-ju had
sufficient influence over her mother to prevent
her doing more.

Blackburn was a genius in his line ; he kept all the strings to his bow and all the arteries of his vast organization under his personal inspection and control. He had found the secret of success, in the path which he had struck out, to lie in universal applicability and novelty. He had boasted that he could furnish, on due notice, whatever the heart of man or woman could desire—whether the customer were a prince or a princess, a dock-labourer or a charwoman ; and he had reclaimed his pledge by providing an elephant within four-and-twenty hours of its being asked for, on one extraordinary occasion. He was proud of his last development in an aristocratic art region. He magnanimously enjoyed solacing the idleness of rich, the sorrows of poor gentility, 'that would never recognise him and his, in spite of his celebrity and wealth, as the equals and privileged associates of its members. He relished highly, as Fouché did, counting in his pay sprigs of the nobility, who were also among the chief purchasers of his rarest and costliest adaptations from Worth.

Iris did not know how much she owed

again to her grandfather and grandmother, when, to her great relief and something like happy bewilderment, she found herself at once approved of and appointed on Blackburn's staff. She was even entrusted with very valuable materials, including an idea with a suitable moral, by a well-known artist, the cartoon to be destroyed as soon as a single copy was worked, of a screen in three panels.

One panel displayed Arachnë in her earlier humanity, carried away by conceit in her weaving; the second gave the cowering foolish weaver-woman brought face to face with the great goddess Minerva, whom she had dared to challenge to a trial of skill; and the third represented Minerva looking down in supreme contempt on the humble spider and her web, all that remained of the presumptuous Arachnë and the product of her loom.

Long afterwards Iris was wont to view that trophy of bold, true, delicate, if formal, lines, traced in softest, richest silks, with many mingled feelings. In the meantime it was a congenial occupation, as well as a bracing effort at independence, for Iris to work faithfully and lovingly at the great artist's fancy.

Iris needed this help for her heart and mind, her faith and patience, while the summer was yet young, since every day the weather was growing warmer and the season drawing nearer to its climax. The garden in Fitzroy Square, which had been a pleasant oasis in the dreary desert of stone and lime when Iris came, became prematurely sere, yellow, and brown in its lack of country freshness, country freedom, country whole-someness, of gradual, bountiful growth and decay. It seemed to miss half the stages of vegetable existence, whether of autumn bravery of colouring, or of a winter robe of spotless swan's-down, instead of a rapidly melting, smutty, grey travesty of snow.

The society of the boarding-house had lost its strangeness to Iris, but it had also become more and more irksome with a constant re-minder that she was out of her element among people whom she neither judged, nor condemned, nor despised, but not one of whom bore much more than a human, national, tolerably civilized affinity to her, in her nature, beliefs, and habits. She had a

notion that she might have fared better in
some of the other houses in the neighbourhood ; especially she hankered after those
that appeared occupied by struggling artists.
But the Haighs held themselves aloof from
Bohemianism in every shape, reckoning on
drawing their clients from more solid and
substantial, if less original and enlivening
quarters ; even Ju-ju only cared for artistic
circles, inasmuch as they supplied her with
canons of taste.

Many of the residents in the house were
going away with Ju-ju Haigh to pay visits to
the sea-side, to Normandy, or the Engadine.
Iris's choice of society, such as it was, began
to narrow just as she had a craving for it to
widen.   She would be left almost alone in the
white dusty streets by the time she thirsted
intensely for a quiet, sandy-coloured country
road running along a reddish, purplish-green
stretch of common or down, the shade of
trees, the cool ripple of water, the yellow
corn-fields ripening to harvest.

The figure of an old woman, loveless and
unloved in her solitary age, sitting at home
in her cheerless great house, or driving out
by herself in her close carriage on her mono-

tonous round, had reproached Iris, from the first, many a time. The reproach was more than half morbid, for Lady Fermor had never shown that she cared for her grand-daughter's company, and she had driven Iris from her, by persecution and panic, which might have worn the girl into her grave, or carried her to a madhouse.

CHAPTER XXX.

IRIS had been out for a little more air and a saunter in the greater space of Regent's Park, when, just as she re-entered the house, she met Mrs. Haigh in such a state of consternation that the girl's roused imagination could settle on no smaller calamities than the kitchen chimney on fire, to the destruction of the eight o'clock dinner, or to the first clerk in the great banking-house having announced his intention to set up an establishment of his own. But Mrs. Haigh speedily undeceived her.

'Oh, my dear Miss Compton, *she* is here! Lady Fermor is here, and I dared not attempt to deceive her about your being with us; indeed, she did not ask; she simply said, "Take me to Miss Compton," and she walked straight into the drawing-room, dismissing

me with a nod, and staring about her without
troubling to return the bows of the assembled
ladies, to whom I gave her a general intro-
duction. They have all left the room, and
she is sitting there alone, for Haigh has declined to have anything to do with her. I
am afraid you must go to her and find out
what she wants. If it is anything reasonable, if she wishes to board here along with
you, I will do my best, though I do not know
if Mrs. Judge Penfold and the rest will consent to be ignored, even by a viscountess—
your grandfather was a viscount, wasn't he,
dear Miss Compton? not an earl, as I am
always inclined to make him—when they
are all private ladies. If she thinks your
board too high, though the times are terribly
expensive——'

'I do not think that will be the reason of
her coming, Mrs. Haigh. I shall go to her
at once.'

The thought of her grandmother away
from Lambford, from which she had not
stirred for a dozen years, had a great effect on
Iris. She felt it when she went into the
drawing-room, where a moderate amount of
second-hand, frequently incongruous furni-

43—2

ture was made to stand for a great deal, and
for the accomplishment of entire harmony, to
which the separate possessions of the different
ladies, with the traces of their various avoca-
tions, lent an additional unhomelike hetero-
geneousness.

Whatever the person most concerned may
have felt, it was a shock to her descendant
when she saw the aged woman rooted up
from all her old surroundings.   Iris had been
accustomed to think of her grandmother as
about as stationary and constant in her attributes and actions as the fixed stars, as accustomed to be law to her house, the author and
ruler of its whole economy, which for that
matter proceeded from her will and existed
for her pleasure.

Therefore the contrast was great of finding
Lady Fermor seated uncomfortably in a chair
which was the opposite of her own at Lambford, with Mrs. Rugely's easel at one side,
and Mrs. Calcott's basket heaped with the
badies' socks and pinafores, which she was
always manufacturing for charitable bazaars,
on the other, and Mrs. Judge Penfold's dog
barking, and Ju-ju's kitten putting up its
tail, as if to assail the intruder.

Iris's heart smote her, and she advanced quickly to her persecutress, crying out :

' Oh, grandmamma ! I am sorry I have given you so much trouble, if you have come up to town on my account.'

' You may be sorry,' said Lady Fermor emphatically, extending two fingers to her grand-daughter. ' I have come a long journey on your account. I am here to fetch you away ; so you had better get ready as soon as possible, and not keep me waiting longer than you can help. The carriage is at the door.'

Iris was taken aback. This was not like the scoffing leave to go which had been granted to her at their last meeting. To return to Lambford, though she had not been very happy in Fitzroy Square, was never what Iris had intended ; all the old objections to her residence with her grandmother, which had grown unbearable, might still remain in full force. The loathed apparition of Major Pollock, of which she had got rid lately, seemed to rise again before her and make her flesh creep. For anything Iris knew he might have come up with her grandmother to London—he might be in the carriage outside, ready to spring upon her, in a figure.

She could not resign herself again to the old tyranny, the old taunts and indignities which had threatened to thrust her on the most miserable fate that could befall a woman ; not for her native air and the place and the people she had known and loved so long ; not for Lucy Acton, who had expressed herself by letter as dubious of the step Iris had taken, even while condoling with her most sincerely on the causes which had led to it, could Iris make so bootless a sacrifice. But the assurance of the shrivelled-up wreck of a woman before her staggered Iris, and caused her to hesitate what to say or do.

Lady Fermor delivered herself of a gesture of impatience, and called out harshly :

'Have I not stooped enough, girl ? Would you have me humble myself in the dirt to tell you I'll never mention poor old Pollock's name to you again ? If you had not been a prim, scared idiot, you would have known it was not in earnest. I have got one of my other grand-daughters, Marianne Dugdale, to be a companion for you. I have taken a house in Kensington, that you may spend a few weeks in town before all the world is gone, in a manner more befitting your antecedents. Afterwards I am thinking of a little trip to Buxton, or Scarborough, or Scotland—I am not too stiff to accomplish it—and let you two girls have the benefit of it. I dare say you will turn up your noses because Buxton is not Spa or Homburg, and Scarborough Compiègne, or any other French place frequented by the ex-Empress, and Scotland Norway. But I can tell you, when I was young, a girl would have counted such an excursion an opening for making her fortune, and a wonderful stroke of good luck.'

'It is kind of you to put yourself about,' faltered Iris, not at all sure how her words would be taken. 'We are much obliged to you. If I could only flatter myself you wanted me—you really wanted me—grandmamma,' said Iris, with a more uncontrollable break in her voice.

'Oh, as to that,' said Lady Fermor, carelessly shaking out her sable-lined cloak, and giving a twitch to the strings of a new and striking lilac satin bonnet, 'I got on very well by myself. You need not flatter yourself that you are of so much consequence. It was Thwaite, who came over and dug into me to go and see after you,' with a keen glance at Iris.

'It was very good of Sir William to think of me,' said Iris simply.

'Oh yes, we're all kind and good now, when you've had your swing, and we're ready to look over and make the best of a girl's incredible folly. Thwaite brought Marianne Dugdale and me to town, but you need not thank him for it. I imagine he has taken a fancy to Marianne, and though she's a goose, like the rest of her kind, she won't be so goosey, perverse, and infatuated as to hold out against lawful authority, and a thousand advantages far beyond what she could hope for. By-the-bye, I hope Marianne's having stepped into your shoes, both with regard to Lambford and Whitehills, will not interfere with your throwing down your arms, and submitting to your natural superior,' wound up Lady Fermor, fixing Iris with a wily, glittering eye.

'No, no,' said Iris hastily, falling into the trap forthwith, lifting up her head involuntarily, unconscious of a bright spot rising on each cheek. 'Why should it? But there are some other things to be thought of.'

'Out with them. Am I to go down on my knees to beg your pardon?' with a feeble movement to rise from her chair. 'I have long thought the world was upside down, and this will only be the reversal of our natural position. Come, let me get over it as soon as possible. I should not mind it, if my old knees were not so rheumatic.'

'Grandmamma, I beseech you don't,' implored Iris, in terror lest Lady Fermor should carry out her horrible mockery. 'How could you think or say such a thing? I only wished to tell you that I have paid my board, but Mrs. Haigh has made arrangements for me remaining much longer. I cannot help disappointing her perhaps, but I ought not to let her suffer otherwise.'

'Humph! very impertinent in her to have anything to say to you at all, and still more impertinent to go on forming plans without consulting your friends, but we must take that with the rest. I'll settle with the lodging or boarding-house keeper, or whatever she is. Any more stipulations?'

'I have taken in work—art-work—from Blackburn's, and I have expensive materials to account for, as well as the piece I undertook to embroider.'

'Good gracious, Iris! were you mad? How could you disgrace yourself and me in such a manner?' cried Lady Fermor, stumbling to her feet. 'You might have gone on the boards with less scandal, if ever such an act of low-lifed absurdity come to light. We must drive instantly to the shop, and buy up all you had to do with—only buying up will stop the man's mouth; and though it were half the shop, the sacrifice must be made. When I engage in a thing, I go through with it. But your vagary is likely to cost me a pretty penny, Miss Compton, in addition to aching bones. You had better think twice; or rather, I hope you will be off my hands before you engage in another. After the good education you had—even though that woman Burrage was a fanatic—to descend to the gutter by taking in work from a public shop!'

'It was plain that in Lady Fermor's old-fashioned estimation, art needlework was not a whit better than white seam ; and she con-

sidered that Iris Compton had let herself
sink, in the course of six or eight weeks, to
the level of a shirt-maker or slop-worker.

It was like a dream to Iris to find herself
snatched away from Fitzroy Square. She
left Mrs. Haigh in a manner consoled by the
spectacle of the coroneted carriage at the
door, and the undying recollection that Lady
Fermor had called in person for her grand-
daughter, though her ladyship had not behaved quite so well on the occasion as might
have been hoped for from a viscountess.
Iris had promised to come and see them all
again. On the other hand, it was certain
that Mrs. Haigh's ladies, though they were
ready to give honour where honour was due,
would not have suppressed themselves to the
extent of being trodden under foot by a titled
sinner.

It was not so much as if the present—it
was rather as if the recent past were a dream,
when Iris knew herself sitting in her old
place, listening to the old high-handed talk
and vituperation that were yet not without a
harsh kindliness, for which they were not at
all indebted to Lady Fermor. They owed
it solely to old home-like associations. But,

as Iris told herself, what could she have done
after the chief grievance was removed, and
her grandmother had bound herself to keep
the peace, than return to her duty, and wear
again the yoke of her youth?

The house which Lady Fermor had taken
off its former tenant's hands, for the last few
weeks of the season, was at Kensington
Gore. It was beyond the precincts of Bel-
gravia, and beyond the Knightsbridge art
studios and the barracks, which, following
the example of the ubiquitous mews, invade
select territories. Its windows did not give
a false idea, as they looked full on the re-
freshment and refuge of the grand old leafy
gardens. The glittering pinnacles of the
Queen and country's memorial to a good
prince, with his other monument, the huge
ugly dome of the Albert Hall, promising un-
limited music, and the pile upon pile of the
second national museum, offering numberless
antiquities, pictures, the Raphael cartoons,
were all close at home. So was the Row,
with its mid-day horses and riders, and so
was Hyde Park, with its afternoon stream
of carriages, and not very far off was the
Broad Walk, that noblest avenue in which

old court beauties, fair French *emigrées*, the world of fashion and letters, once came to see and be seen, to sun themselves, and shine as lesser luminaries, reflecting welcome rays on the obscure world crowding to gape and stare at the town lions. There was the plainest of brick palaces winking and twinkling with its many white-faced windows in the sun, or looking grim and uncompromisingly prosaic in the shade ; but never to be forgotten in its lack of all architectural stateliness and beauty, because there the great ones of other generations, kings and queens, statesmen and generals—not lost among starched and soulless court officials— had been born, or died, or had spent, in the glare which surrounds a throne, some of their brief fateful days.

Iris had never before lived in such a charmed region, where the hours might well seem too short for the attractions which claimed them ; but she hardly noticed it at first, she was so full of excitement and anxiety about her cousin, Marianne Dugdale. The relationship that connected them, to which Iris, in the absence of nearer kindred, might have felt fain to cling, had been marred by old sins and sorrows. These transgres-

sions, poor faithless souls feel tempted to
fear, are more frequently visited on innocent,
sensitive victims than on guilty, callous
culprits.   But when it comes to that, the
vicarious suffering may be the most powerful
means of saving the sufferers from the trans-
mission of the moral taint.

Lady Fermor had been plagued by few
scruples in calling this other grandchild to
her side, but Iris retained a pained recollection of what her grandmother had said with
regard to the light in which the Dugdales
and the Powells must regard her, Iris.   They
might owe some charity to their grandmother, but they owned none to her.   She
was only a rival claimant for Lady Fermor's
bounty, the grand-daughter of the man who
had foully wronged their grandfather.   It
was a case of family guilt and alienation
which could hardly be repaired even between
the harmless representatives of succeeding
generations.

CHAPTER XXXI.

MARIANNE DUGDALE.

ANY faint hopes of amnesty which Iris might have entertained were extinguished; her face fell and was dyed with a crimson blush of shame and confusion, at the reception she met with from Marianne Dugdale. The young lady had been riding with some country companions who had turned up in town, opportunely for her. She had come back almost simultaneously with her grandmother and Iris, so that Miss Dugdale was still standing in the hall, holding up her habit with one hand, and releasing herself from the burden of her hat in the hot weather with the other, when Lady Fermor called out, 'Are you there, Marianne? Come here; I have brought you Iris Compton. Let me see if you two cousins have any look of each other.'

Marianne turned round and showed a short but well-balanced, well-carried figure; a face from which all the dusky, not particularly tidy hair was swept back from the good forehead; a pair of the darkest brown, keenly enquiring, nay, haughtily challenging eyes; an ivory complexion, as if pale with passion; a straight nose; a mouth so shaped to pout that one could hardly conceive it pacifically straight, or drooping lugubriously at the corners.

Marianne Dugdale was one of the pale roses so much in fashion, well set in thorns, if ever rose were so set. She made a queer half-mocking little bow, touched the tips of Iris's fingers with her own, and saying decidedly, 'There is not a shade of likeness between us, granny,' turned away and ran lightly up a flight of stairs.

'How she detests me, at first sight! Though I cannot help it, I need not wonder at it.'

Iris took the manner of the reception to herself, in distress and humiliation, and asked in nervous apprehension with what show of friendship and enjoyment the two could live together, and go out together, certainly for the next month or two, possibly for years ? She would have repented quitting Fitzroy Square and returning with Lady Fermor, if her grandmother had not come for her, made terms with her, and, as it appeared, constituted it Iris's duty to submit.

For half a week Iris remained disabused of the impression that she was an object of half-righteous, half-vindictive abhorrence to Marianne Dugdale, who was watching everything Iris did and said with a hawk-like alertness which Iris felt far transcended her own mortified well-nigh timid inspection of her cousin.

The first thing which shook Iris's belief in her kinswoman's *rôle*, as a small black and white Nemesis, was Iris's observation of the inherent youthfulness which clung to Marianne Dugdale. Iris knew they were much of the same age, but she had been feeling a woman for years now; she was certain she presented no such juvenile traits as were constantly peeping out in Marianne Dugdale, and largely qualifying a nature that even in early womanhood was sharp, shrewd, and full of self-reliance. There was the oddest mixture, the result of early forcing and contemporaneous neglect, of strength and weakness, boldness and shyness, confidence and distrust, tenacity and collapse, in the little square-shouldered person who was to divide with Iris the claims of the young ladies of the family and the filial duties of grandchildren to Lady Fermor, both in the house at Kensington Gate and elsewhere. The double temperament and training betrayed itself even in Marianne Dugdale's physique. Her little chubby hands were dimpled like a child's, and while they were tolerably useless in some things—notably in woman's work— in others they displayed the dexterity of an intelligent mechanic. The owner of the hands had been very irregularly educated, but she had a scientific, particularly a mechanical bias. She preferred mathematics and chemistry to history and literature, while she had a side for fiction and poetry; with a greater resemblance to men than to women in this respect, she relished an opportunity of working with wire and wood; she bored and whittled like a boy; put all the bells right in the house at Kensington Gore without the assistance of a workman, to the amazement, amounting to consternation, of the strictly conventional London men-servants and maid-servants ; rectified the unevenness of various articles of furniture, and set straight every picture that was hung wrong by a hair's breadth.

Her voice, in the style of her hands, was furnished with a singular variety of tones, some of them strident and self-assertive enough, others—mostly addressed to children and animals—were wonderfully winning and sweet, full of childlike vibrations, and an irresistibly coaxing ring.

But Marianne Dugdale's attitude to her grandmother, Lady Fermor, was the most puzzling and characteristic of any. In one sense the girl openly defied the formidable old woman, and took the control of herself, Marianne Dugdale, into her own hands, where she had been early accustomed to keep it. She proposed to do in London and at Lamb-ford exactly what she had done in her father's country-house, in the depths of Devonshire—and that was very much what she liked.

In another sense, the strong, ardent re-joicing youth of the girl had an underlying fund of generosity and pity for the old

woman's position, fighting against infirmity
on the brink of the grave. After a conspicuously self-willed action or flippant speech,
Marianne Dugdale would suddenly turn, as
if moved by a different spring, and speak the
gentlest words she had uttered that day,
refrain from resenting a jeering rejoinder,
refuse to be held back by any chilling re-
pulse, decline to quail or to recoil passionately from offering to the stout-hearted,
thankless rebel against her own needs and
other people's devices, soft, cherishing aid.

Iris looked from one to another in marvel
to see how Lady Fermor would stand it—
the open, scarcely seemly contradiction—the
sudden sweet, tender amends ; and if anybody had presumed to observe and applaud
the relenting, the likelihood was that Marianne Dugdale would have gone off at a
tangent—harder, sharper, more dogged than
ever.

Lady Fermor's looks and words offered a
new field of conjecture to Iris. There was
a strange, suspicious forbearance and ob-
liviousness about Lady Fermor's dealing with
Marianne Dugdale's behaviour, which Iris
suspected was made up of new sensations—

considerable amusement, and an abiding conviction that in spite of all the restiveness
and waywardness, she, Lady Fermor, was
mistress of Marianne Dugdale, and could
easily crush her opposition whether in great
matters or small. There was no coherence
as yet in the warring qualities in the girl's
disposition, no principle of steadfastness to
enable her to pull herself together and resist
any impulse, whether for good or evil, ad-
visedly and to the end, no outward abiding
support. She was physically fearless to
daring, but it remained on the cards that she
might prove morally weak as water.

Iris was not thinking of herself, but she
was as a still, deep stream, obeying a great
law, which, however ruffled, could not be
diverted from its course and was full of
reserved power.

Marianne Dugdale was like a brawling
brook, spending itself in foam and noise,
rushing hither and thither, in wandering
channels, either to lose name and identity,
or to discover itself suddenly turned aside,
and notwithstanding its raving, carried where
it would not, to turn some wheel, form some
reservoir, or serve some foreign purpose for

which it had not the slightest inclination. Iris arrived at the sound conclusion that, however indifferent or even averse to her a girl like this might be, it was hardly probable that she would figure in the light of an avenger of hereditary injuries. Marianne was not made of the stuff that constitutes an old supporter of the Vendetta, or a modern Nihilist.

It was on the occasion of Lady Fermor's persistently twitting Iris, according to an old bad habit, which their recent compact had not interfered with, that Marianne Dugdale abruptly declared herself on the side of her cousin, called her 'Iris' in those accents which, when they were friendly at all, sounded as if they came fresh from a warm, true heart, and might wile a bird from a tree. She walked over to Iris's side where she sat in one of the windows looking out across the crowded traffic of the road to the grand alleys of the gardens. Marianne knelt, or as she would have called it, in her scorn of sentimentality, 'plumped' down before her cousin, leant her crossed arms against the frame in which Iris was working at the Arachnë, amidst altered surroundings, and began to chat over the events of the day in which the girls were mutually interested.

The action was the nearest approach to a caress in which the least caressing of girls was likely to indulge. It was also a pretty, unaffected movement, at once confidential and implying more or less voluntary allegiance.

Iris welcomed it gladly, and with as much cordiality at it was wise to display to a wild bird that might take alarm and start off on the smallest provocation.

Lady Fermor had never known the love of woman to woman, and had been as incredulous of it as many men are, or pretend to be. She had never looked upon her own sex otherwise than with a mixture of dislike, suspicion, and contempt, as natural enemies and rivals, or as poor inferiors. She now regarded the little group before her with a snort of exasperated scepticism. 'Well done, young ladies!' she said sardonically, as she rose from her chair with an effort; 'the pose is very pretty, but it is wasted upon me. You ought to keep it for *les jeunes ingénues* like yourselves. Oh dear, no!—don't, I beg of you, disturb yourselves on my account,' as

she stumbled and recovered herself on the
way to the door, and both of her grand-
daughters were starting up to her assistance.
'I hear Soames coming to tell me I ought
to be lying down ; but if she proposes to hug
me, or even to kiss my hand, I'll dismiss her
on the spot. I make it a principle not to
encourage humbug.'

'"Don't be too affectionate, Charlotte, or
I'll kick yer,"' Marianne quoted audibly from
'Oliver Twist.' Then, as the door closed,
she appealed to her cousin. 'Now, Iris,
you've known granny a great deal longer
than I have ; but I have seen enough of her
to dare you to contradict me, if you are in
the habit of speaking the truth, when I say
she is an abominable old woman.'

Iris looked down into the clear, searching,
imperious eyes fixed on hers, then before she
answered looked away into the green gardens. Happy little children played there
from morning till night. Invalids in Bath-
chairs were pulled along that the sick folk
might look with their dim, faded eyes at the
sunny sky and the flowery earth, and know
summer had come again, and dream for a
brief moment that health and strength were

not fled for ever, but might return once more.
Men of business, pursued by cares and worries,
undertaken for women and children, trudged
home from their offices. Those mature pedestrians, who ought to have known better,
fondly persuaded themselves that they had
found a natural refuge by choosing, in preference to the rattle of vehicles and the constant
interruptions of the streets, this comparatively quiet ground, with the grass beneath
their feet and the trees above their heads ;
but the deluded men only used their leisure
to think the more of the business they had
meant to leave behind. Lovers sat on the
benches, and looked into each other's eyes,
and exchanged a word now and then, as if
they had sat there since the gardens were
opened, since Adam and Eve walked in the
garden of Eden, and could be content to sit
there for ever. Iris left her needle sticking
in her work, clasped her hands, and spoke
piteously :

'She belongs to other times and other
manners, so that we cannot judge her and
her temptations. She has lost all she
loved and honoured, and she does not care
any more for love and honour.' Her voice

fell as if this were, what indeed it was, the crown of human wretchedness.

A passing shade of awe crossed Marianne Dugdale's dauntless face, but she did not refrain from proclaiming triumphantly : ' Then, Iris Compton, we can be friends. I agree with what you say. She is a miserable, old, old granny, and sometimes I would give anything to help her. But I was trying you to see if you were goody-goody, as she said. She told me it was because of your goody-goodiness you ran away ; and if you had begun to preach to me about reverence, and the duty and privilege of respecting and loving that dreadful old woman, though she is a poor old soul all the same, to whom we have the misfortune to be related—I should have given you up at once, since I won't be preached to. Luckily, granny, however horrible otherwise, never tries on that : and, like her, I make a principle of never encouraging humbugs.'

' Everybody is not a humbug who does not go about proclaiming all the truth, who even keeps back as much of it as is possible sometimes. You would not expose a wound to shock your fellow-creatures,' remonstrated Iris.

'No—yes. You are talking of a different thing. I shall always speak the truth—I have never told lies. I should not know how to hold my tongue. And you—you were not altogether silent in your conduct; I mean when you ran away. Ah! I have you there, Iris.'

Iris winced before this very plain speaking. 'I thought I was forced to leave grandmamma,' she said, 'but I did not go clandestinely. I dare say she told you that also; for whatever she has done, she is a truthful woman, Marianne. It was not a pleasant experience. I do not like to speak or think of it, and I do not care to speak ill of Lady Fermor when I am eating her bread. Remember, she has brought me up. I have lived with her all my life, as you have not done.'

'The more shame to her, then, to speak to you as she did a little while ago—as she is constantly doing,' asserted Marianne Dugdale roundly, 'and the more fool you to let her. I shan't run away, see if I shall. I shall stay as long as she will keep me, or till I make the place too hot to hold me, since I have come to granny, though I hated the thought, for the good of the other girls, and because papa scolded and mamma cried about our poverty. But she shan't take me off, or put me down, or domineer over me, you notice, Iris. I will manage better ; and neither shall she ride rough-shod over you any more, if I am here,' declared Marianne, in the tone of a gallant little cavalier who means to fight in defence of his lady. 'You are really a great deal too good for her, instead of thinking only of yourself, and preaching to every other person in the goody-goody fashion I feared, and have been looking out for, every day since you came. But it is not true ; you are quite an honest, reasonable, jolly girl. I shall do what seems best to me, and you will do what you think proper, and if granny will only consent to behave herself tolerably for an old woman, we'll do all we can for her.'

'I am much obliged to you, my dear cousin,' Iris was forced to laugh, 'but you must not mind me. Lady Fermor and I understand each other, and I am not often vexed by what she says. People at her age are privileged. It is only her way of joking. You must mind yourself. You may not find

it so easy for you as you suppose, though I
need not say I will do all I can to help
you.'

'I do not see how there can be any difficulty,' said Marianne, a little offended in
her extravagant independence and self-con-
fidence, as she rose to her feet and prepared
to stroll away. 'I have always got my own
way, at least almost always. Papa is constantly up to his ears in business, and a very
bad business it is with the agricultural interest gone to the dogs. Mamma is too lazy,
and reads too many novels to take the
trouble to call me to order. She never had
a mother of her own—at least the one she
had was as good as none; and her father
was soured with his misfortunes, so that her
spirit was broken when she was still a girl;
but I am not going to lose my spirit. The
other girls, Cathie and Chattie, are younger
than I am, and I rule them instead of their
ruling me. There are the boys, to be sure,'
said Marianne, with a momentary pause.

'I thought you had no brothers.'

'Oh no! not brothers, but as good—
rather better—five cousins; Tom and Ned,
and Dick and Harry, and Charlie. Tom

and Ned are going to India, and Dick and
Harry are at Cambridge. Dick is to be a
barrister, and Harry an engineer. Charlie
has had thoughts of the Church. The rest
of the boys say he has plenty of "jaw" if
his mind were made up, but I don't believe
he ever will make it up. My mind is made
up that he will choke on the Thirty-nine
Articles. He is the only sop among our
boys, and he is dreadfully spoony on Cathie,
which is a great bore both to her and the
whole of us; to me more than anybody else,
for I was understood to look after them and
keep them from running into mischief—at
least till Sir George came home.'

'What a responsibility!' exclaimed Iris,
with proper sympathy; 'and who are all
these boys you have on your mind?'

'Of course sons of papa's brother, Sir
George, out in India. He has been a widower
ever so long, and sent all the boys home
when they were young to papa and mamma's
care. She and papa were glad to have them,
both for their own sakes—since boys are so
much nicer than girls, and because their
father, Uncle George, is a great swell in the
Civil Service, who can not only make good

allowances to his sons, but is coming back to
provide for us all when his time is out ; only
he may die, no doubt, or marry again, or do
something out there before he is able to
think what he is about. I have been a great
deal more with the boys than the girls.
Even Cathie, the sister next me, is three
years younger than I—a soft little mortal,
who can't say "bo ! " to a goose or to Charlie.
I flatter myself I *can* play cricket, and take
a fence, and drive, and row, and chaff. Boys
will chaff and criticize, but I didn't often
give in to them, I assure you.'

These were advantages of education of
which Iris could not boast ; before which,
with their results, she must often sit dumb,
though she had not been used to regarding
herself, or to being regarded by others, as
a particularly weak and helpless young
woman.

CHAPTER XXXII.

THERE was a budding phase of life of which Iris in her isolation had known little or nothing. Except at the Rectory, she had scarcely come into familiar contact with a gay, accessible, yet engrossed and restless group of young people like herself. And at the Rectory, life had consisted simply of a family party, into which Iris was admitted by special favour. It was her fortune in the weeks spent at Kensington Gore to form one in a cluster of young people of more varied elements, not related, not like, for the most part only recently known to each other, yet who seemed suddenly, in spite of what might have been regarded as insurmountable barriers, to wax well acquainted, and to a certain extent intimate. The result was produced largely by the freemasonry of youth, and by

a certain simplicity of character which distinguished more than one of the number.
Perhaps something was due also to that
curious fusing influence of London, or any
other great city, on individuals who, however
dissimilar otherwise, resemble each other in
having been brought together unexpectedly,
in coming from other spheres, in being
strangers together in a new field, making a
common experiment in a complex, manifold
life. The group was so far well matched that
it consisted of two girls and two young men
—Iris Compton and Marianne Dugdale, Sir
William Thwaite and Ludovic Acton. He
was doing nothing more heroic at this time
than studying the science of the sea and its
ships with their work and warfare, at Greenwich Hospital, converted into a college for
aspiring able-bodied lieutenants, as well as
for more juvenile naval recruits.

Iris and Sir William Thwaite met as friends
of old standing, and they also met more as
contemporaries and equals than they had ever
done before. Iris had fallen into the habit,
in the past, of classing him among middle-
aged and elderly people, even while she
had felt inclined to coach him and lend

him her countenance in seeking to serve him. Doubtless this was the consequence of his real and supposed disqualifications for figuring among the young people to whom the Squire of Whitehills should have belonged, and of the gravity and formality of manner conspicuous in a man bent on fulfilling his obligations to society, while very doubtful of his power to fulfil them.

It surprised Iris to hear Marianne Dugdale, who, after she had found her tongue, was frank and free in expressing her opinions on every subject, mention Sir William casually as ' a nice young fellow.'

' Oh! I know what you are thinking of,' Marianne cried, in answer to Iris's bewildered look. 'He was not always a gentleman, and he made a foolish marriage, and went to the bad for a time. I know all about him,' continued Marianne, who had a mania for universal knowledge and capability, and was apt to leap to the conclusion on slender premises that she was mistress of both. 'But what of that when he has redeemed his character? Down where I come from we would say he could not help the first, and he was very much to be pitied for

the second. Men are not perfect. If they
are manly, honest fellows, and do their best,
we need not wonder though some of them
have a fall or two. We may be glad when
they can pick themselves up again, as they
do after a spill in the hunting-field, and be
ready to lend them a hand, and expect them
to give us another if we come to grief. Oh !
we are not so starched and severe, and, upon
my word, I do not think we are the worse
Christians for it down in my part of Devonshire. Neither are we such prigs of scholars
or such very fine ladies and gentlemen as to
refuse to forgive a man for a false particle,
or even for a verb or an adjective out of
joint, or because he keeps on his hat, or
does not take off his muddy boots, or bolts
his knife, or puts his feet on the chimney-
piece—not that Sir William Thwaite commits
these enormities to my knowledge ; I merely
used the similes to give point to my asser-
tions. What would a host of them signify if
he were a man and a gentleman at heart, as
I am sure he is ? Yes ; I know all about him,
and I say he is a nice young fellow, fairly
handsome, with a fine carriage. He is not
stupid a bit, for he has told me ever so many

things I wished to hear about India, where Tom and Ned are going.'

Iris remembered Sir William's passing another examination in reference to India with great credit.

Whatever Marianne Dugdale had learnt she had certainly not been informed, for whatever reason, that the Squire of White hills had been a rejected suitor of her cousin's, an amount of ignorance for which Iris was devoutly thankful, and which she earnestly trusted would receive no enlightenment.

Lady Fermor had made a supererogatory statement that Sir William entertained a fancy for her other grand-daughter. Marianne, on her part, openly professed an interest in him. Iris, too, had an interest different in origin and kind, which included thoughts of poor Honor Smith, and a wonder whether *she* were altogether forgotten. Iris tried to look at Sir William in a new light with impartial eyes. He was certainly a young man, not over thirty, although he looked old for his age. Strong and comely, in spite of a certain wayworn look, a trace of trouble, a shade of sternness, which lent him a kind of dignity. Yes, there was a homely dignity about him; and his manners, though these were blunt and unsophisticated, were no longer laboured and artificial. He had ceased to think of what had become in a measure habitual to him. Other and infinitely heavier considerations had totally outweighed social dogmas, and from the moment that he had regained his liberty in this respect, the man and the gentleman at heart shone out in his words and actions. Where there is no longer anything to conceal, and not a grain of pretence, there may still be rusticity, but there is no room for vulgarity and pettiness.

> ' Heated hot with burning fears,
> And dipped in baths of hissing tears,
> And battered with the shocks of doom
> For shape and use,'

Sir William was a rustic gentleman, but he was not unworthy to rank with the best, not the worst, of the class to which he had risen. Iris was able to comprehend how a young gentlewoman, a little rustic herself, rather masculine, after the fashion of the generation, in temper and training, with a natural impatience, and scorn of forms and ceremonies and nice outward distinctions, should fraternize with a Sir William, and hold him in sincere esteem, even in high regard, in defiance of what carping people persistently remembered and chronicled against him.

It was impossible for Sir William not to respond within limits to the generosity and kindness of the girl, as he had done long ago without bounds in more difficult circumstances, to the generosity and kindness of another girl. It was therefore quite true that he was on very good terms with Marianne Dugdale, to the extent of submitting to be chaffed by her, as if it were a pleasure to him, and of bluffly chaffing her in return, as he had never dreamt of chaffing Iris Compton. It was perfectly possible that something—a great deal—might come out of these terms.

But Iris soon discovered that another puppet was to play his part in the little drama, a puppet with such strength of feelings, hopes, and wishes, that he threatened to produce a serious complication of the plot. Ludovic Acton had been at Greenwich before the date of Lady Fermor's arrival in London. He had been commanded both by his mother and Lucy to call immediately on his father's most difficult parishioner. Being greatly

under female commanders from the moment
he put his foot on shore, he had reported
himself at Kensington Gore before Iris was
transplanted there. He had done it in the
way of duty, and with the usual failure of
poetic justice in the affairs of men, in the
very act of filial, fraternal, and neighbourly
goodwill he found himself, as he had soon
to own with a groan, 'completely done for.'

King Lud had happened to pay his first
visit when Lady Fermor was not out of her
room, and he was handed over to a wonderful dark-eyed girl, with a little mouth, a
square chin, a square yet symmetrical figure,
altogether, habited in a sort of workwoman's
blouse, in which she did not seem to feel the
least put out. She stepped briskly from the
conservatory, where she had been knitting
her brows, and pouting her lips over the dila-
pidated rock-work, the rolled-up tarpaulin
which ought to have shaded the roof, the
syringes which would not spout water, the
sickly plants ravaged by the green fly. She
scarcely waited to hear his name, and to
listen to his modest explanations and apologies
for intruding on an unknown young lady,
before she told him:

'Oh! I know who you are' (it is a wonder she did not say, 'I know all about you'). 'You are the son of the Rector down at Lambford. Your people said you would call, and I am glad, because sailors are handy, and you may be able to help me. Come and see the disgraceful wreck of a London conservatory.'

King Lud went and saw and worked with Marianne Dugdale for half an hour, and did not conquer, unless in the trifles of nailing up some of the higher dropping-down cork rock-work, erecting the tarpaulin in its proper place, clearing out the pipes of the syringes and playing them on the astonished green fly. As if that were not enough for the entomological specimens, Marianne gave her order, 'Smoke, Mr. Acton—smoke!" It was like the royal child's command to the wise and witty author of the 'Three Estates,' 'P'ay, Davie Lindesay—p'ay!'

King Lud, too, complied forthwith, consoling himself for having to light and puff a cigar in such a presence by the true conviction that those pretty fresh lips, frank and fearless as they were, had never been soiled by so much as a cigarette, for the country

Amazon of high degree is more innocent and unsophisticated than the same Amazon belonging to the town. He was conquered himself, hard hit, beaten to the wall at the first bout. He had never seen such eyes, or worked in company with such clean baby fingers. He had never met a girl so genuine, so original, so unconscious, so bright. He might have added he had never been so warmly congratulated for small achievements, or so soundly rated for sundry little mistakes—in the height and flutter of his admiration, in fastening the cork and the tarpaulin.

In his entire subjugation her Majesty's officer called again at Kensington Gore on the following day, under the poor pretext of renewing his smoking operations against the green fly, which the butler could do more effectually than a visitor could manage it. On his second call Ludovic saw Lady Fermor, and she who had never been deficient in hospitality to young men, made him free of the house during her stay in town. She did not withdraw this permission, as she might have done, when she found that the Rector's son availed himself of it on every possible and impossible occasion, until his visits to town must have made a tremendous inroad on his studies at Greenwich. In fact it came to this, that King Lud, who had been heretofore the most diligent and devoted member of his profession, appeared to be living in the College at Greenwich for the sole purpose of paying court to somebody in a house at Kensington Gore.

Lady Fermor was very old, but she was neither blind nor deaf to the extent of the infirmities interfering seriously with her intercourse with her followers. She was not a fool, and she had other plans and projects for her grandchild; but she was 'a cool hand' and a bold player. She was fond of a fair field and no favour in the game of life, and it is to be feared she had downright satisfaction in making mischief between men and women. She let Ludovic Acton call or come to dinner or form one of the escorts to the girls as he and they chose. Lady Fermor let Marianne Dugdale talk to the lieutenant by the hour, satisfying her inquisitiveness, which was immense, about all the ships he had been in, and all the service he had seen, about the North Sea and the Coast of Africa, and the dockyards at home, about his experience of the different modes and rules for cricket and foot-ball and lawn-tennis.

Lady Fermor never interfered. She seemed to suffer the young people to take their swing in the easiest, most inconsiderate manner. Yet when Iris came to think of it afterwards, she could not recall one occasion when the old woman, apparently doing nothing, had not so held the shuttle and chequered, twisted, turned back and directed anew the threads which were to weave the pattern in the web of destiny, that Marianne Dugdale, who imagined herself a free agent, did not stay at home when she had promised to go out, walk with Sir William when the arrangement had been that she should walk with Mr. Acton; did not wear the one man's flowers and sing the one man's songs when she had accepted the other's bouquets and undertaken to warble his ditties.

The policy might be Machiavellian, yet it was simple enough, and it had a foundation prepared for it in a headstrong girl, calling out for her own way and getting it, but swerving aside and giving in because she had still those troublesome commodities—a conscience and a heart, not to speak of a suscep-

tible vanity and a temper even more susceptible and easily played upon. She had
also a large supply of what old-fashioned
books call 'frowardness,' which owned no
control, and could be reckoned on to influence Marianne according to the principle on
which some pigs and donkeys are driven, if
one may be forgiven the inelegance of the
simile—start them with their faces due north
and they are safe to back due south.

Still more ready-made material for an
enemy of Marianne Dugdale's to employ to
her detriment, was to be found in the fact
that she was a born coquette—born, not
made—above all, not in deliberate, guileful,
perhaps mercenary practice, which constitutes
all the difference in the world. Without
doubt, her rearing among the tribe of boys
who were as good as brothers, yet who were
not brothers, gave early stimulus and scope
to the bent; for she liked attention, not from
one squire alone, but from all who came
within her orbit. Without thinking what
she was doing, without any conscious motive,
especially without a set aim to an end, Marianne had an instinctive, exquisite enjoyment,
inscrutable to Iris, in smiling and frowning,

praising and blaming, pleasing and teasing, coaxing and vexing—as the waters came down at Lodore—now Sir William, now Ludovic Acton. This was done in a manner calculated to set the two young men, who had always been on civil terms, and when left to themselves were growing friendlier every day, as much by the ears as if they had both been their tormentor's devoted slaves.

That one of the gentlemen was Marianne Dugdale's devoted slave neither she nor anyone else could long deny, while she was inflicting alternate ecstasy and misery upon him. But jesting at scars because she had never felt a wound, Marianne did not mind the responsibility in the least ; if anything, it added zest to her entertainment. Thus she never ceased laughing at poor King Lud's moon of a face and his tow-coloured hair, apparently without any clear and forcible conviction that these not strictly picturesque attributes belonged to a brave, honest gentleman on whom it was a shame and disgrace for any woman to inflict an unnecessary pang.

In her thoughtlessness, her gaiety and kindness degenerated into careless selfishness and positive cruelty. Iris could utter no protest, though her heart waxed hot within her, because there were considerations which stopped her mouth, and because Marianne would not be preached to, and must be taught neither by precept nor example, but by what is frequently the grimmest, as it is certainly the most efficient teacher of all, bitter experience. Hers was really a fine, open, even loyally affectionate nature, but in the meantime it was in a state of chaos, not cosmos. There was no reign of duty in the soul, no supreme sovereignty tending to bring every thought and affection into noble subjection. There was no leading, binding, restraining principle in her life, though she had been baptized and confirmed, and called and believed herself a Christian.

It was a lively surprise to Iris at first, when King Lud presented himself day after day at Kensington Gore, without a single musical instrument in his pocket, when he was punctilious in never asking for music more than once in the twenty-four hours, since Marianne Dugdale, though she could sing like a lark when she chose, was only moderately fond of the joyous science, and had been heard to speak disparagingly of musical men.

Accordingly Ludovic Acton was resentful to the verge of repressed fury when Iris referred without malice to his stock of musical instruments, and expressed innocent surprise that he no longer cared to accompany anybody on the piano. 'Why did you say that?' he took her to task as if she had been one of his sisters, and with as much indignation as if she had accused him of conduct unbecoming an officer and a gentleman. 'I am not fonder of music than other fellows.' Then in answer to her 'Oh, Ludovic!' 'I mean than other fellows who have idle time on their hands, which they do not well know how to get rid of. I say, Iris—Miss Compton—it was rather nasty of you—I mean it was hard upon me, to bring up that about my flutes and guitars. I am sick of them, and shall have a private sale the next time I am afloat. You have heard her—Miss Dugdale—laugh at cater-wauling fellows, and no poor beggar likes to be an object of ridicule in his set.'

The abandonment of the former ruling passion in favour of a far mightier, of one of the great fulcrums which bend and twist the human heart, so that vestiges of its work often survive all else—even the object which

called it forth, struck Iris as a most formidable
symptom of poor King Lud's fatal malady.

The season was approaching its close when
Lady Fermor came up to town, and she made
that an excuse for no formal bringing out of
her grand-daughters. However, they came in
for the fag-end of the gaieties, which were
still fresh and agreeable to them. Country
neighbours of Marianne Dugdale's fortunately
in town, one or two Eastham families that
had condoned Lady Fermor's offences long
ago, supported the two girls, stopped them
when they were driving with Lady Fermor
in the Park, offered in the persons of the
matrons to chaperon the cousins, and invited
or procured invitations for them to the last
plays, operas, flower-shows, breakfasts, and
balls. These invitations, by Lady Fermor's
desire, included Sir William Thwaite and Mr.
Acton.

The girls were called upon to wear their
pretty demi-costumes, their daintiest walking
array, with bonnets which were little more
than coronets of flowers, parasols which were
mere handfuls of lace, and gloves that were
buttoned to the elbow and beyond the elbow,
and yet were the most fairy-like gloves in the

world. But what was the effect of any walking garb to the shining or gauzy evening robes with more flowers, the hair turned back or in little waves as usual, in the most natural and quietest fashion, but for the diamond band or the diamond stars which flashed out from the red gold or the dusky brown little heads !

Lady Fermor not only grudged none of these expenses, she ordained they should be incurred, and evinced a certain cynical satisfaction in hearing that her two fair young grand-daughters formed an admirable contrast to each other.

Iris waltzed again, as a matter of course, with Sir William, and if either remembered the former occasion he or she made no sign. It was no business of hers, neither did she know it at the time, but one of the balls happened at a great house which had given a similar rout years before, when a member of the present company had stood among the rabble round the door and envied the very footman whose flesh-coloured calves were so much at home on those stairs, and asked despairingly whether he could ever be at ease in such regions ?

Now, so far as that went, he was as undisturbed in mind as when he traversed the old
barrack-yards, and sometimes Iris Compton
hung upon his arm, but the spirit of the dream
was changed.

In addition to a taste of the good things
of the season, there were many sights for
Lady Fermor's young people to see, and this
business they prosecuted with commendable
assiduity and considerable satisfaction. The
last would have been still greater if there
had been no such disturbing element as the
rival claims of Sir William and King Lud,
with the rapidly developing moon-struck
madness of the lieutenant.

Still these were exacting, engrossing hot
days and nights when there was always
something to be done which could not be
put off, whether it were an excursion to Kew
or Richmond, an old-fashioned survey of
the Tower or the Mint or the Mansion
House, services at Westminster or St. Paul's,
visits to the Ladies' and the Strangers' Galleries
in St. Stephen's, an enterprising hunt for
old china, dawdling at Morris's or Burnet's,
distributions of prizes for window-gardening
under difficulties, mornings at the crack

training school for nurses, the Hospital for
Incurables, the last best crêche. It was a
marvellous jumble, and though Iris was
tempted to think the unlooked-for holiday
was alloyed by the sport which Marianne
Dugdale could not resist making with her
two Samsons, perhaps without it the whirl
would have lacked some of the eternal
play of human passion and warfare of
mortal life. There would have been a
certain spice to the intercourse absent if it
had not been for the sentiment that mani-
festly pervaded the contending factions. To
say nothing of the under-currents which
might be doing their own work, there was
something rousing in the spirit of indignation which filled Iris when she saw one
or other of the victims specially ill-used.
There was zest for more than one person
in every event likely to satisfy the craving
curiosity to know beyond mistake whether
or not Sir William and Marianne Dugdale
were merely playing parts at Lady Fermor's
instigation and under her influence, whether
the play might not grow second nature and
end in earnest, whether Marianne's maiden
meditations were still as fancy free as she

46—2

professed, or whether they pointed to the
well-endowed Baronet or to the poor naval
officer.

Marianne had made one sacrifice for the
sake of her family, but those who argued,
from that event, that she would make another
and greater, on her own behalf, did not
understand the girl. She was more likely to
act on a whim, an impulse, a chance—as Iris
never could have acted, and possibly repent
and cause another to repent at leisure, for
the rest of her life. It was likely to remain
an unsolved problem to the last moment
what Marianne Dugdale might or might not
do.

Iris, without a severe analysis of motives,
without outspoken confidence as yet even
between her and her old playfellow King
Lud in his need, acted as consoler to each
of the young men in turn ; for wounded pride,
and mortified masterfulness, and sheer irrita-
tion caused by an exasperating process, require soothing, as well as outraged love.

But Iris was angriest and sorriest for
Ludovic Acton. Sir William might put in a
claim as having borne the brunt of repeated
disappointments and trials, but he had learnt

at last to wear a calm front to the world.
And if he were proposing again to marry on
the prompting of a third person, after all he
had suffered, because a suitable alliance was
desirable for a man in his position, then there
was a good deal that was incorrigible in his
conduct which, though it encountered loss,
could not command sympathy.

Sometimes Marianne took it into her un-
accountable vagrant fancy to take umbrage
at all the three others, and would as good as
quarrel with them so far as they would let
her. She would withdraw herself as much
as possible from association with them, go
about her own business and leave them to
bear each other company and get on as well
as they could without her.

It was then a pitiable case with the poor
fellow who gave himself up to uncalled-for
self-reproaches and desperate apprehensions
because of his mistress's inexplicable displeasure. But in spite of his groans, there
was a considerable amount of fraternization
between the deserted members of the party,
and a good deal of pensive and humorous
enjoyment — not so much in airing their
grievance, for they were too true and too

much inclined to be attached to Marianne
Dugdale to take that course, but in enduring her capricious humour and the temporary
banishment, if not from her actual presence,
from her goodwill and merry conversation.
When the affair was hopeless the company
would let her go off by herself, as she insisted
on doing, to secure friends for whom she would
flaunt a preference that passed away soon.
The trio would bring themselves to obey her
literally, and let her alone, stamping about
the back drawing-room or sulking in the
conservatory, while those in disgrace would
linger apart in the farthest window, or would
pluck up a spirit and take it upon them to
get their hats and stroll across the road to
the adjoining gardens. There the three would
walk up and down beneath the trees, carefully
keeping in sight of the house lest Marianne
should return to her right mind in a twinkling, as was her wont, forgive them in a
body without telling them their offence, and
come out after her brief eclipse, the blithest
of them all.

The promenaders would talk Lambford
and Eastham assiduously. It was then that
Iris found out how Sir William had come to

know and to love every hazel copse and
sunny sloping field and rushy brake on
Whitehills. She and Ludovic, who had been
brought up in the parish, were not better
acquainted with its dear old holes and corners
and fonder of them than this comparative
new-comer. Neither could she fail to perceive, little as it was intruded on her, the
interest he had learnt to take in the people,
especially in those who were most dependent
on the consideration of their neighbours, how
much sympathy he had for them, what good
sense and good feeling and dry humour into
the bargain he showed when he talked of
them, how attentively he listened to every
suggestion on their behalf.

And how many notable books he had
been reading ! Books of which King Lud
had not even heard the names, books which
she had longed for, but had not yet been
able to procure. To think that Sir William,
to whom she had tentatively lent 'Tom
Brown's School Days,' in connection with
whom she had not been without thoughts of
adding to the other book 'The Water Babies'
and 'The Heroes,' by way of tit-bits to encourage a literary appetite in its infancy,

should have got in advance of her here, as
he was before her and King Lud in sundry
original, intelligent investigations he had
instituted, mostly in the track of natural
history! His occasional half-eager half-
thoughtful references to those experiments
sounded as if he might live to attain some
distinction among the students of nature.

What advances he had made in true manhood! How he was casting off the slough
of the lower animal! How fast he was
growing in his solitary life at Whitehills!
What would Honor have thought of him if
she had lived to see him now? Ah, poor
Honor! her life could hardly have been his
gain. Her death was part of his emancipa-
tion. But if she saw it all from beyond the
golden gate, from within the silent land,
where she might have found Hughie Guild,
and be walking with him by the water of
life, would she not be more than content?

CHAPTER XXXIII.

GREENWICH AND THE ACADEMY.

KING LUD was almost frantic with delight on account of an ovation which was to be paid to him, not by the multitudes of the city, which his great namesake is said to have founded, but by two or three quite private and obscure persons, one of whom, a square-shouldered little individual, with a strong dash of the child still in her wilful girlhood, had turned the unfortunate fellow's head. His friends, with Marianne Dugdale among them, were to go down to Greenwich to spend an afternoon there under his leadership and drink tea in his room. Lady Fermor declared herself equal to the effort, even though it had been a dinner in the Trafalgar, a great deal better than the Ministerial white-bait dinners, such a dinner as she had been accustomed to attend at least

once or twice in the season, both there and
at the Star and Garter, Richmond, with
shady cronies whose disreputable names
were no longer heard, while happily the very
scandals in which they had figured were fast
being forgotten.

The day was as fine as could have been
wished for ' a family party,' as Lady Fermor
called it, complaining that there was a danger
of its being as dull as family parties generally
were.   They drove down to the dirty little
old town of Elizabethan and naval memories,
and made their way to the grand terrace
before Queen Mary's and Sir Christopher
Wren's Hospital, which time's changes have
converted into a college.   Everybody's
spirits rose.   How could he or she help it
under the inspiring influence of the blue sky
and the wide flowing river—the great watery
highway to the largest city in the world?
The widening mouth of the English Thames,
which, though it is little among its mighty
brethren the Volga and the Danube, the
Ganges and the Euphrates, the Nile and
the Niger, the monster Amazon and Mis-
sissippi, yet bears upon its breast such a
huge and precious burden of traffic as they

never knew. A brown 'streak' turned up
with silver, it swayed and rippled and
throbbed, with its fringes of tall masts and
flapping sails, from Gravesend to Wapping;
its Isle of Dogs converted into a custom-
house station; its Deptford ringing with
hammers as when Peter the Great riveted a
bolt there; its Woolwich Marshes bounding
the Arsenal, where Woolwich infants are
cradled and rocked. Barges laden with hay
and coals crept lazily along with the sunlight
red in their umber-coloured sails. Steamers
churned the water as they darted by, puffing
out grey smoke and wreaths of white vapour.
Here was the column erected to the gallant
young Frenchman Bellot, who earned the
gratitude of a foreign nation by the fruitless
attempt to discover its lost heroes beyond
the terrible barriers of everlasting snows and
huge glittering icebergs. He left half his
tale untold, but there was a living man—
sandy-haired, moon-faced, large-limbed,
standing there, among the everyday group,
who, if he were permitted to leave out his
own doings, could add something to the
fascinating ghastly story.

Within the big-domed building was the

Painted Hall, with the portraits of all the
Captains bold of whom the best artist in each
man's day could leave a token.   There were
the reflections—often with the show of their
ships at their backs—of Drake and Blake,
Rodney and Anson, Cloudesley Shovel and
Benbow; and in a shrine by himself the
various representations of ' Harry Bluff,' of
whom, when he was a fearless middy, the old
salts had sworn,

> 'One day he'd lead the van ;'

and here he was, from the maimed lad still
foremost in the fray, to the man with many
orders on his breast dying in the cockpit of
the *Victory.*

As if these were not mighty names enough
to conjure with, and pathetic stories sufficient
to melt the hardest heart, there were the
weather-worn, far-borne, simply tragic relics
of the last holocaust to the spirit of the North
Cape, the sad trophies brought back by Dr.
Rae : battered spoons with familiar crests
and initials, a watch long stopped, torn leaves
from a Bible and from Oliver Goldsmith's
sweet old English inland story, in which
there is no echo of the thunder of the surf,

and little more travelling, after all, than what
is chronicled in the first chapter of the book
of the change from the Blue Bed to the
Brown.

For once King Lud was the most favoured
of men in his surroundings, and he rose to the
occasion. He descanted, all the more tell-
ingly that it was with modesty and sincerity,
on the true glory of his profession, its adventures, exposure, self-denial, and self-sacrifice.
Who could think of the advantages of a good
English estate, even of a fine old English
manor-house and an ancient title, at such a
moment ? Not Marianne Dugdale, who was
entranced with all she saw and heard, until
she envied the little boys climbing the rigging
of the training ship and the very invalids
in the floating hospital of the *Dreadnought.*
She had the different parts of the vessels, the
science of their steering, the method of their
logs, the movements of their compasses explained to her. She did not tire of hearing
the curious details of their flags and signals ;
she was not at rest till she had walked across
the park where Greenwich Fair was wont to
be held, as far as the Observatory, to have her
watch set by the great dial, and she honoured

the lieutenant by appointing him to conduct the operation. Iris and Sir William were strolling among the English elms and Spanish chestnuts, past the railed-in stump of a tree garlanded with ivy, which is said to have been a stripling when William and his Normans conquered Saxon England, to One-tree Hill, in order not to miss the second of the three finest views of London, rising dimly out of the haze and extending in a grand sweep from the water-towers of the Crystal Palace to those cupolas of Sir Christopher Wren's, while all the time the faint hoarse murmur of the terrible mill which grinds, not corn, but human hearts and brains, was heard without ceasing, uttering its fit accompaniment to the scene. As for Lady Fermor, she was long ago under the sleepless guardianship of Soames, being made as comfortable as circumstances would permit in the lieutenant's room.

King Lud might live to perform more lion-like actions than he had yet accomplished. He might be a full-blown admiral, with his sandy hair powdered with white, while he halted on one knee after the fashion of Horatius Cocles, from spent shot or baser rheuma-

tism ; but it was hardly likely that he would
ever spend a happier afternoon than that
which Lady Fermor and her party passed
with him at Greenwich.

Everybody awarded a tribute of praise to
the owner of the room in the Hospital College for his expert contrivances where space
and convenience were concerned. Everybody turned over his books and admired the
flowers—Kent dahlias and gladioli, fragrant
jessamine and heliotrope, with which Ludovic
had promptly provided himself to do honour
to the occasion, and to dispose lavishly on
every side, in order to embellish his plain
bachelor's quarters and poor lieutenant's
equipage.

Sir William Thwaite leant his back against
the chimney-piece, thinking honourably and
humbly how nice and pretty it all looked,
wondering how Acton could manage it, if he
were naturally 'a dab' at arranging his cabin,
or if the inspiration came with the visit of his
queen to his small lodging. He—Sir William—did not believe he could have done
anything like it, to save his life, with all
the will in the world, and the accumulated
materials at Whitehills. The only time the

place had been *en fête* in his day, Sir John's
widow was in command, and she had produced nothing so spontaneous and refreshing
as this ; but it was too late to take a lesson.

Lady Fermor had the seat of honour—the
single easy-chair in which the lieutenant was
wont to lounge, smoke, and read—nod, Marianne Dugdale alleged.

The two girls lingered by the high window
looking down on the water, with its never-
ending charm.   They were dressed alike in
stuffs of the dusky-red colour which fashion
has called in to take its place, by way of contrast, among the pale and neutral summer tints
of the last decade.   The dark red is especially
welcome with the first breath of autumn,
when all nature is ripening and mellowing to
richer, deeper dyes.   The girls were as deco-
rative as the flowers, and for that matter
they had taken what they liked from King
Lud's abundant treasures.   The primrose
and orange nasturtiums, white jessamine,
and purple penstamens, culled from the lieutenant's improvised beau-pots and posies,
came out with charming effect against the
Venetian-red background—so did the shell-
pink of Iris's cheeks with the golden-bronze

of her hair, and the creamy-white of Marianne's skin with the mouse-brown of her 'top.'

The little sobering sense which was left in
King Lud was all but ravished from him by
Marianne's gracious offer to make tea, assert-
ing brightly that it was just like doing it for
'our boys at home,' and summoning him, as
if he had been her special boy, to stand at
her elbow with the camp-kettle—in itself a
pleasant curiosity to her.

The close and collapse of the gala—for all
happy things come to an end here, and not
a few of them, alas! collapse in the very
process of enjoyment—was brought about
by the intervention of Lady Fermor. Even
she had been taken captive for the moment
by the fresh, heroic, homely elements of the
entertainment, to the extent of being subdued
by them for a little while. But when the
party were taking a final saunter down the
Painted Hall, in which the shadows were
gathering, so that the painted warriors were
growing obscure on their stations, and only
one flaming yellow and red picture, indicating
a ship on fire, stood out from the dull darkness of the others, like a portent of evil,
Richard was himself again.

Marianne Dugdale was walking as if in a dream, wonderfully silent for her, with her brown eyes a little downcast, beside Ludovic Acton, who, though he wore no uniform, seemed for the moment transformed—sandy hair, shyness, softness to women and all, into one of the heroes on the walls stepped out of the canvas, reflecting glory on one proud girl by his notice.

Lady Fermor was stamping along by the aid of her stick on Marianne's other side. Suddenly she raised her harsh, highly-pitched voice, and at the same time cast a meaning, satirical glance at her grand-daughter. ' I think I miss a picture which ought to have been here too—that of blubbering Black-eyed Susan, following her truant " sweet William " on board the fleet in the Downs.'

Marianne started, wide-awake, flushing to the roots of her hair. ' Oh ! she was an odious creature,' she said. ' Thank goodness, she is not here. Indeed, I think a sailor should have nothing to do with miserable whimpering sweethearts and wives. His ship should be his mistress, as a priest should be wedded to his flock.'

' My dear Marianne, I never knew you

had adopted the doctrines of the Roman
Catholic Church,' remonstrated Iris, laughing at her friend's vehemence, and feeling
for King Lud, at once lifted from a pinnacle
of exultation and dashed into the depths of
despair.

His very rival commiserated him. 'I
thought blue-jackets carried all before them
when they went a-wooing,' said Sir William,
without any suspicion of cynicism.

'They are no better than red-jackets, or
any other jackets,' answered Marianne rather
testily than with an implied compliment.

Very likely she had forgotten Sir William's
former connection with the army, and in good
truth he had no reason to recall it with pride;
but the most sensible men are silly on some
points, so he blushed a shade with gratification, though he maintained magnanimously:
'You don't mean to say any woman could
have resisted the French chap commemorated
out yonder, or the boy whose statue we saw
in marble, the great statesman's son, who
spoke of his mother and his native town,
and how happy they would be to welcome
him home, when he lay a-dying through
volunteering to carry succour to the forts in

the rebellion ?   That was before my time ;
but I've some notion what it meant.   Sup-
posing either of them had lived to come
back and lay his laurels at a woman's feet,
do you suppose she would have spurned
them ?'

'The laurels have to be gathered first,'
said Marianne drily ; 'and when I come to
think of it, I am sick of what people call
"the pomp and circumstance of glorious war."
What did all these battles and all these
bloodthirsty commodores and rear-admirals
come to ?—I mean what lasting good did
they do, unless to their blustering, strutting
selves ?   Who were really the better for
them ?   I believe it would be easier to say
who were a great deal the worse.   What
hearts they broke !   How many widows and
orphans they made !   I think I shall go in
for the Quakers and the bloodless victories of
peace.'

'But some men must fight that peace may
be preserved, and the helpless defended from
injury,' remonstrated King Lud, recovering
from the vicious snub administered to him,
with the attendant amazement and discomfiture.   'A sailor's life is far from all

fighting, especially in these days. Our
squadrons lie along many a shore to check
more powerful rascals than slave-dealers.
We crush, in their infancy, aggressions and
outrages to which the barbarities of the slave-
trade are a trifle—short in time and limited
in extent.'

'A sort of water-police,' said Marianne
contemptuously.

'And sailors are still finding new lands
and helping to civilize wild states,' suggested
Iris a little injudiciously.

'Not in my opinion,' alleged Marianne,
with her neat little nose in the air. 'My
conviction is, that frigates and gunboats float
about in disgraceful idleness, in order to
keep up the taxes, which papa is always
groaning over. Besides, we must maintain
a navy which is no longer wanted, in order
to provide genteel sinecures for the younger
sons of gentlemen—fellows who cannot get
along on shore. For my part, I would rather
herd sheep in Australia or hunt ostriches in
Africa, or turn a vulgar, respectable shop-
keeper at home.'

The attack was so outrageous that it
became laughable. The eclipse of the sun

might nevertheless have come to one person through a girl's spirit of contradiction and craven susceptibility to ridicule.

But to the others the sun declined in its ordinary fashion as they skirted the shoulder of Blackheath with its girdle of villas. It was a mere sunset, but it was such a sunset as the neighbourhood of London renders unrivalled in its kind. Iris was compelled to acknowledge that the misty flats of Eastham, or of Holland itself, for that matter, could do nothing to those marvellous shades of saffron and gold, faint coral, dusky sorrel, the dim lilac of the autumn crocus, and a grey steely blue. Was there something human in the pathetic glory of the skies above the great city of vast wealth and grinding poverty, foulest sin and fairest righteousness, many crimes and many sorrows, much nobleness, much holiness, and much innocent, grateful gladness? Did the groans and curses, tears and sighs, smiles and laughter, go up from tens of thousands of hearths to paint themselves in that solemn, subdued glow?

The Academy was not yet shut; and out of many visits one stood out in the remembrance of the little company that so often met together in these weeks. They had all been tolerably united in their criticism. They had agreed that English landscape-painting held its own as in the days of Gainsborough and Constable and old Crome ; that the mantle of Sir David Wilkie still fell, here and there, on the painters of the ruggedness and the humour, the exquisite tenderness of peasant life with its homely affections. These were no more sordid and petty now, to the hands that could draw and the eyes that could read them, than they were nearly a century ago to the brave, gentle son of the Fife manse, and his enthusiastic admirers. Heroism quailed a little before the cynicism of the generation, but picturesqueness and passion made a vigorous stand against the learned affectation of burning incense to colour and form alone—colour and form without a soul human or divine, or else with a soul rejecting all humanity as devoid of dignity and interest unless it came in the shape of pagan Greek myths and Roman crimes and feasts, sensuous and sensual, petrified in their passion, cold in their exaggerated repose, because the faith and heart

of man have alike forsaken them, and they
live only as carefully conceived, exquisitely
executed conceits and richly decked phantoms,
dragged painfully from a past which, having
no parallel in the present, can scarcely be
regarded as the type of the life of all the
ages.

One at least of the visitors was sorry, with
a yearning regret and a shamed mortification,
that the sacred art which once made Italy,
Flanders, and Spain glorious—on which men
spent their lives—into which they could then
throw their hearts—was so feebly and scantily
represented in Christian England. Iris was
inclined to ask, 'Will there come a renaissance
here also ? and will the Christ on His cross,
the Virgin Mother, and the noble army of
martyrs replace once more Apollo and Venus
with their votaries ?'

Most people will allow that it becomes in
time weary work for eyes and brains to study
even the flower of the year's pictures. It
will be so even when the much-tried and
abused hanging-committee have done their
duty perfectly, in which case there will cease,
no doubt, to be painter hermits and mis-
anthropes, Timons of Athens in art, who

decline in savageness or scorn to permit the
muddle-headed, vulgar-minded public to gaze
on the artist's transcendent, mysterious
achievements. But it is not so universal an
axiom to the many, it may come with a
shock of surprise to some, to learn that it is
possible for bodily fatigue to end in crossness
of temper even with the young and strong,
the ardent and intelligent. For that matter,
still more with the young and strong than
with the middle-aged or the old and feeble,
who have been compelled to bear the brunt
of many a burden—be it a pleasure, and to
feel the weariness of life even in its most
enjoyable hours.

Will it be believed that Marianne Dugdale,
after having entered with much enthusiasm
on this as on other rounds, by the time she
felt a falling to pieces of the backbone, a
heaviness and ache of the brows, a slight
swimming of the eyes, and giddiness of the
brain, was about as much out of humour as
could be said of an impatient-tempered girl
who, if she were not arrested in time, would
develop, without fail, into a hard as well as a
true, a fiery no less than a warm-hearted,
vixen ?

'What !' does anybody ask ; 'is it possible
that such an ill-bred, captious girl, who
played with a gallant, modest gentleman's
devotion, and ungratefully turned upon him
in the height of his happiness, spoiling it
utterly that afternoon at Greenwich, can
still have " followers," in the vulgar sense of
the term, and fast friends worthy of the
name ?'

In the first place, there is an undeniable
and a piquant stimulating charm—to begin
with, at least—in the natures which are rarely
two hours alike. Such dispositions appeal
at once to the pride and to the chivalry of
certain men, to tame the shrew, and to save
her from the tyranny of her humours. These
consist not infrequently of the heady efferves-
cence of good qualities suffered to ferment and
run to waste—hatred of dissimulation, indignation at injustice and wrong, strength of attachment to another person, violence of disgust
with one's foolish self. Above all, Marianne
Dugdale's present companions possessed the
touch-stone which could go beneath the
surface and penetrate to the core of her
character. They looked on her with kind,
friendly eyes, and could not help being fond

of her. The two men and the woman knew
it was only fair to recognise that if one of
them had been evidently more tired than the
girl was, or had met with the slightest accident, or had become suddenly a little ill, or
even had been merely old and tottering like
Lady Fermor, whom her grand-daughters
had no cause to love and honour, Marianne
would instantly have come to the front like
a heroine, would not only have borne any
suffering of her own like a martyr, but would
have died sooner than confess to such suffering.

As it was, however, Marianne commenced
to snap up her companions' harmless remarks
and execute half-comical, childish growls at
which no one ventured to laugh, to flout the
others, to flounce about by herself.

Soothing was tried in vain, compromises
were disdainfully rejected, proposals to bring
the day's visit—the final visit to the Academy
—to a summary close scouted at, humble
suggestions of an adjournment to the refresh-
ment-room for a glass of claret and a slice of
chicken, or a cup of tea and a stale bun,
treated as a positive insult. When it came
to this pass, Marianne's adherents drew dis-

creetly apart, freed her from their observation, and sought to occupy themselves with what remained of their morning's work. Only King Lud was too miserable to accomplish the assumption, or practise the restraint of indifference. He feared his mistress might be ill, for it was quite possible that Marianne would only display her bodily distress in this perplexing, mental fashion. He knew at least that she was unhappy for the moment, and he could not endure the thought of abandoning her to her unhappiness. He followed her at a respectful distance, patiently waiting for any sign of relenting and recovery, when he would gladly take upon himself the blame of having been stupid, tiresome, and positively cruel in inciting an unfortunate girl to do too much, and exert herself till she was half dead.

Iris and Sir William were together at the farther end of the room. He was pausing and brightening at some Indian scenes, showing his companion where the cane-brake or the mangrove swamp was trustworthy or at fault, explaining the native costumes and indicating the castes. He stopped at the occasional portraits of military officers as pointedly as if he were going to salute them, and became excited and exultant over the likeness of one who had been a chief in Sir William's campaign. It was clear that he bore no malice against the service, that the disgrace with which it had threatened him had faded away from his mind, from the time that he had confessed and acknowledged the justice of the sentence. It was possible that in place of being humbled by the stripes torn from his arm, the ignominy of the lash hanging over his head, and the expulsion from the ranks in which he had risen to be an officer, it was the scar on his neck and breast, and the sword-cut across his arm, which for a moment burnt again with the proud consciousness that he too had been a soldier, and had fought and bled for England and his colours.

Unexpectedly the couple came upon a picture hung low which they had not observed on their previous visits. It was not a striking picture in size and situation, or in more than a moderate degree of artistic merit. It was the subject which arrested the two gazers, paled their cheeks, dimmed their eyes, brought a quiver to their compressed lips. The

painter unknown to fame had represented a
drowned woman, washed gently enough on a
pebbly shore by the rippling waves of a sea
no longer raging in the fury of a storm.
The limbs, those of a fine, strong young
woman, were disposed decently and peace-
fully, as if a friend's hand had laid them to
rest ; the face turned up to the summer sky
was unmarred in its still serenity. The head
lay cushioned, as it were, on the wealth of
brown hair which had broken loose and
streamed like so much seaweed back from
the bare brow and blanched cheeks. So had
Honor lain on the Welsh beach. The
thoughts of both of the spectators flew back
to the disaster. Then the attention of the
pair became concentrated and fascinated
by a likeness—a double likeness. It was
not wonderful that with their minds full
of a similar catastrophe and its victim, Sir
William and Iris should see a resemblance
to the late Lady Thwaite in everything, save
in the rich warm colouring which, to be sure,
the cold sea and colder death had already
stolen from her cheeks and lips before the
husband was called upon to identify the
body of his wife. But there was no reason

why either of the two, looking fixedly and silently at the picture, should simultaneously, as if by contact of thought, detect traits the same as those with which they were familiar in a living face in that very room. Sir William and Iris had never before compared Honor Smith to Marianne Dugdale. Size, colouring, circumstances, were all so different, that the comparison sounded absurd even now; yet there were the friends of both making it decidedly and unmistakably, until the eyes which had been averted looked into each other and claimed the wondering admission.

'You see it also? Poor Honor and Miss Dugdale!' exclaimed Sir William, half under his breath; 'I never once thought of it before.'

'Nor I,' responded Iris, as low as if she were exchanging secrets with him.

They did not say another word. She glanced at him and seemed to find a shadow of half-superstitious awe on his manly, ruddy face. Was he revolving the curious unde-fined law, that what has been shall be again, on which gamblers base their calculations? The unexplained but acknowledged fact that, in the history of men as of nations, events often repeat themselves, against all reason, against all warning, in a mysterious, well-nigh gruesome fashion ? Was he judging rashly that it was vain for him to struggle against his fate ? Did he seek to persuade himself that in this direction, after all, might lie at once the atonement for his past errors, and the building up of a new and higher character ?

When Iris and Sir William rejoined Marianne Dugdale, she had so far come to herself as to suffer the companionship of the faithful lieutenant, and was no longer treating him worse than dog or mouse before she could consent to dote on him for ever. But the union was not indissoluble. Sir William Thwaite approached her with a forcible appeal and a pathetic reverence expressed in an eager concern for her welfare.

'Are you tired out, Miss Dugdale ? will you not allow me to find a seat for you ? I will manage it, never fear, though I have to turn out by force that stout old gentleman, and that puppy-dog of a lad on the next sofa. I see you have your fan, let me fan you. I have a long, strong, steady arm ; I could work a flail or a punkah without much effort. After you're a bit rested and refreshed, we'll drive straight home and do no more to-day.'

Thus the girl was caught and transfixed by the change from simple friendliness and from the half-frank chaff, the half-sparring flirtation into which Marianne Dugdale would have beguiled a man engaged the day before to the object of a lifelong attachment, or a colonial bishop just consecrated and on the eve of starting for the most murderous of half-heathen dioceses.

Iris knew that Sir William was moved by the recollection of his dead wife, whom he was confounding in a manner with Marianne Dugdale. But Ludovic Acton had no such clue to the problem. He was compelled to believe that his passive rival had suddenly become active and dead in earnest; while he was at the same time—from the support of Lady Fermor, doubtless—so well assured of the success of his suit, that he was already appropriating the tone of an accepted, privileged lover. He was proceeding to take care of Marianne, control, and even gently reproach her, in a manner which she would certainly not have stood from another person, however much his unbounded devotion might have entitled him to forbearance.   But, alas, alas! Marianne was not offended or aggrieved in this instance ; she smoothed down her ruffled plumes, and submitted with a good grace to be looked after and comforted.   She glanced with shy, puzzled inquiry into Sir William's intent face.   Her compunction for something like a child's naughtiness, her swift brightening up again were for Sir William and not for King Lud.   She was a woman, therefore she was caught by novelty and mystery ; she was a woman, so she was fickle as the inconstant wind.   She looked ready to be wooed and won by the altered aspect of the suitor whom Lady Fermor had provided for her grand-daughter, as King Lud had known all along to his sorrow and dread.

CHAPTER XXXIV.

LONDON was fast becoming a high-class social desert, a hot wilderness to be abandoned to its tradespeople and its poor; even they were contemplating excursions to Margate, and tramps to the hop-gardens.

Lady Fermor was about to carry out the second part of her programme, and to save her from the danger of being left to the insipid society of two 'bread-and-butter misses,' she settled that she could journey by short stages as far as the neighbourhood of the first Scotch moor with unlet shootings to which the young men in her train might be induced to accompany her. No doubt Ludovic Acton was in daily expectation of an appointment to a ship, and might have to leave on a moment's notice, but in the meantime he served as well as another. The old despotic schemer, whose

48—2

excess of worldly wisdom sometimes led her
astray, was of opinion that the poor lieutenant with his frantic passion, at which she was
able to jeer and laugh, served in some degree
as a foil and stimulus to Sir William in what
must prove his suit.

King Lud had not given up in despair.
No man worthy of the name will easily do
so, when the prize to be resigned is the centre
of his fondest hopes and aspirations.   He
had fallen out and made it up again with
Marianne Dugdale many times since the day
at the Academy.   He was still not without a
lingering hope that the privilege of travelling with her might do something for his
cause.   At least, it afforded desperately delightful opportunities for being at once the
happiest and the most miserable fellow in the
world—happy with a delirious satisfaction in
the mere consciousness of being in her presence, of watching her and serving her—
miserable in knowing how soon the close
proximity to bliss would come to an end any
way, and what a grievous probability existed,
that by indulging his inclinations and feasting
his passion, he would only reap additional disappointment and wretchedness in the end,

when the suspense was over, Marianne was Lady Thwaite presiding at Whitehills, and he a broken-hearted lieutenant far at sea.

In the beginning of the trip, King Lud's star was in the ascendant. Marianne was radiant and gracious in the enjoyment of all the pleasurable excitement and constant change of scene characteristic of an excursion such as she had never taken before. Since it was conducted to suit the requirements of a woman of Lady Fermor's position and age, there was not the slightest strain on any young person's powers. Indeed, Marianne used her Englishwoman's privilege of grumbling, simply because she had that most charming of all adventures of a phaeton running in her head, and was possessed by a rueful persuasion that she too could have driven many a mile under sunshine and shower, and the merry moonlight; and if she had not been equal to playing on a guitar and singing appropriate songs under difficulties, she would at least have been quite fit for the gay scramble at bezique, and the judicious balancing of two encroachers on her freedom at the end of the day. But even a journey

in first-class railway carriages by short stages
was not to be despised, when the destination
of the travellers was the land of the mountain and the flood, of romance and canniness.
The shortness of the stages and the breaking
of the progress by a day's rest occasionally,
to enable Lady Fermor to dine deliberately
at her usual hour, to go to bed early and rise
late, in order to recruit her forces, also permitted exploring strolls in every direction,
and subordinate excursions in the interest of
the younger members of the party. Thus
the banks of the Severn were visited, the
ancient streets of Chester perambulated, a
raid made into North Wales, and merry
Carlisle with its castle and cathedral learnt
off by heart. The travellers were then not
far from the Scotch Borders, and the final
halting-place, the heathery wells of Moffat,
did not lie much beyond the Marches. But
unluckily, Lady Fermor caught cold, with a
little cough, which teased her in the next
stage of her journey, so that she adopted the
resolution of stopping short and staying for a
couple of nights at an old-fashioned inn, in
which she recollected having been fairly served
many years before. It lay at the junction of

the sister countries, and had originally stood
on a great coach-road, a good deal frequented
in its time. But since the establishment of
railways and new routes, and the withdrawal
of the coaches from the old tracks, nearly the
whole of the traffic had departed from the
place; still the old inn stood, and continued
a house of lodging and entertainment for man
and beast, on a new foundation, its later
energies having been directed to affording
board and lodging to families seeking a
summer retreat, and to furnishing a resort
for the anglers who frequented the 'becks'
and 'burns' in the vicinity.

Lady Fermor declared that her old, plain,
comfortable rooms, which were fortunately
vacant, had not fallen off appreciably, and
that she was satisfied she could have all she
wanted, till a little rest enabled her to get rid
of her cold.

It was a matter of congratulation to Iris
and Marianne especially, that they should
make this halt in an out-of-the-way corner, and
begin their acquaintance with Scotland by
an entrance which might be made on foot,
and was not much frequented and rendered
beaten ground to the destruction of all origi-

nal traits and native simplicity and individu-
ality.

As for the male animal, usually so impatient of delay, and restive under what is a
purely soothing and agreeable element to the
female, the two young men were in that
normal condition which occurs or ought to
occur to a man only once in his life.   They
were at the beck and call of the women ; the
young fellows were meek and docile, ready to
assent cheerfully to any arrangement, eager to
display themselves in their best colours as
they would never be again.   For anything
more, Sir William showed himself less drawn
to Marianne when she was full of glee and
enthusiasm, than when the shadow of a
trouble, however groundless and self-made,
hung over her.   He left her to a considerable
extent to enchant or plague King Lud, who
was thus still hovering on the confines of
gaining or losing the prize of his life, while
Sir William nursed Lady Fermor, made his
own observations, or walked about soberly
with Miss Compton.

There was something of quaint dignity in
the rural aspect of the inn.   It was a steep-
roofed stone house of considerable preten-

sions. The walls were rough-dashed and whitewashed, and further covered by honeysuckle in blossom, and the first 'red red rose' of Scotland which the English visitors had seen. They were told the house was an old Border mansion-house, much more recent in date than the crumbling grey towers and towns they had recently seen in Cumberland, but still old enough to have been beheld by Prince Charlie, had he looked that way in his memorable marches to and from Carlisle. The house stood in a rough paddock, shaded by a few gnarled old trees, and the whole lay in the shelter of the four sentinels—Skiddaw and Scafell rising to the south, with Criffell and the Lead Hills starting up to the north.

The party had private rooms, and so did not come in contact with possible dukes and probable bagmen, chatty or frigid, kindly or selfish old and young ladies. But Iris and Marianne made their own of a modest yet frank young chambermaid, the daughter of a neighbouring Scotch ploughman. She had lived all her life in the vicinity, and could tell her eager questioners the local names and identify to their satisfaction the merest purple crown of every peak and the misty flash of all the 'wan waters' far and near. She was more intelligent than the generality of her compeers in England—the three hundred years or so of parish schools in Scotland having had their effect on the brains of the population. She took evident pride in her birthplace and country, and proceeded, on a little solicitation, to pour forth all the old stories which had gathered round a famous locality.

'It was a weel-kenned part aince, mem. A hantle bonnie English leddies and wilfu' English lads sought it out; whiles there were Scotch leddies and gentlemen came in secret, as far as the bounds o' Dumfriesshire and Kirkcudbrightshire, and rode cockin' awa' in braid day. But there was nae need-cessity for the like o' them taking sic a tramp; they just did it to be neebour-like. What for did they come, young leddies, are you askin'? Losh! div you no ken this was ane o' the toons*—my faither ay maintains it was the chief—where rinawa' marriages were ca'd

---

* The term 'toon' is used freely in primitive Scotch for any better sort of house—farm-house or mansion-house—as well as for a 'burgh-toon.'

aff, the knot tied and the couple buckled, so that neither faither nor mither, nor law-lord, nor minister o' the kirk, nor the king hissel' could rieve man and wife asunder again.'

'Oh, how nice! how funny!' cried Marianne, 'that we should have come by chance to such an inn! Tell us about these runaway marriages, Jeannie. Did any happen in your time? Did you ever see one?' while Iris prepared to listen with interest and amusement.

'Weel, I cannot just say I have, mem,' Jeannie was forced to admit, a little crestfallen at having to fail 'fine, lichtsome English young leddies' in such an important particular as would have been supplied by her having been an eye-witness to the deed, and so able to give personal evidence with regard to all that happened. 'Leastways I have never seen sic grand turnouts as I have heard my faither and mither, and still mair, my grandmither—wha's living to this day with a' her wits aboot her—crack about to their cronies mony a time. Sic marriages hae been going out o' fashion amang gentlefolks for mair than ae generation. But I hae seen a wheen ploughman billies, after a hiring-

market, the warse o' drink for the maist part,
and as mony tawpies of field-workers —
bondagers, folk ca' them here—and servant
lasses—they werena nice—gang afore auld
Fernie who had learnt the trade when it was
flourishin', and still wasna unwillin' to win a
shilling or twa by trying the auld trick,
though the ministers on ilka side, o' a' de-
nominations, are wild now against it, and
fit to rug the head aff onybody that does
siccan work. And, mem, it wasna a' fun,'
continued Jeannie solemnly, for like a good
conscientious lass she was exercised in mind
by the minister's condemnation, every time it
recurred to her memory. 'Fule lads and
silly lasses have been carried aff their feet, and
had to find them again an' rue their madness
ower late. I hae seen a puir lad that wasna
villain enough to forsake even the licht lass
that hadna been ill to coort, and was his
marrow from the moment they had joined
hands, come up next morning, a' shakin', to
the farm-toon where I was living in service,
to seek his wife, an' hae to be telled whilk o'
the glaiket lasses was she ; and I mind a daft
lassie fit to greet her heart oot, because she
had to gang her wa's—for life, mind ye, mem—

wi' a lad she neither kenned nor cared for, seein' that she had only drawn up wi' him the day afore, for naething save to vex her ain lad, whom she had quarrelled wi' nae further gane than the market mornin'.'

' Ah, that was bad !' said Marianne, disappointed in her turn. ' I am afraid your ministers are right, and runaway marriages are not what they should be.'

' Weel,' said Jeannie, with her *amor patriæ* and her Scotch logic resisting even her loyalty to her minister, ' I'm thinkin' there's something to be said on baith sides. The brawest bridegroom I saw here was nae mair than a writer laddie, an' he ran awa' wi' his auld maister's dochter—a lassie wi' siller. But her faither was dead, and she was a saft snool, and had a lang-headed brither who wanted to keep the siller in the family—that was to him and his bairns—sae he was guardin' her day and night an' would hae hindered her frae being married ava ; and they said the writer lad, whether he had the siller in his ee or no, was douce and decent, and would be gude enough till her—far better than her ain flesh an' blude. Noo wasna that a deliverance wrocht by a rinawa' marriage ?' demanded Jeannie triumphantly. 'My granny minds o' a sair fracaw aboot a wicket yerl whom naething would serve but that his genty* bit dochter should marry as auld an' grand and wicket a sinner as hissel'. Her true love wouldna see the shamefu' sacrifice, sae he up and fled wi' the lass. He was a sailor or a sodger lad—ane o' the twa, I forget whilk—a bonnie, brave young man, and he brocht the lassie here. They had but to say twa words to be beyond the power o' ony faithers, to belong to ane anither as was ordained, so that she could follow the drum or sail the seas wi' him, and only death micht part them.'

'Come, this is better,' cried Marianne, with a bright colour in her pale cheeks. 'Tell us more about it, Jeannie. What excitement there must have been! Did the couple come dashing up to the door, their horses covered with foam, and the parents and guardians in hot pursuit?'

'Na, that wasna the way ilka day. Sic wild wark and desperate risks were not tried often, though I hae heard o' horses bein' shot dead frae the foremost carriage, and drivers

* From the French *gentille*.

bribed to lame the puir senseless beasts, or to tint the road and whummle ower their cargy in the middle o' a peat bog, that took ilka man, that tried to stand up, to the houghs in water-holes, wi' nae means o' gettin' on, except by shank's naigie. But whiles, as in the story I'm tellin', the faither was sae close that the lovers daured nae drive up to the front door lest they should be owertaken afore they were made one. They left their empty chaise in a dip o' the road mair than a mile awa', as gin there had been a break-down. The driver galloped on his best horse—and they said it cast ilka shoe within the mile—to gie warning here, while the pair turned into a road—Cambus Road—and jinked by a foot-path to the auld Cambus doocot, that as a' the world kens is jist ower the Borders. There was in this parish a mass-John—that I suld be so far left to mysel' as to gie him sic a name, for he was a godly minister o' the gospel, in days to come. But he didna set his face against rinawa' marriages in his youth, for, licensed and placed though he was, he liked a ploy wi' the lave. What suld hinder him frae hurrying out to meet and marry the lad and lass in the doocot, as gin they had

been twa doos ? They were yoked thegither
as sure and fast as if they had been a leddy
and gentleman surrounded by a proud and
blithe wedding company, in a fine house,*
and blessed by a man wha had maybe chris-
tened her and catacheezed him. The driver
and the leddy's-maid, wha had come wi' her
mistress, served for witnesses. There was a
wild set at Cambus Ha' at the time, but they
were aye hearty and hospitable, and were
gude to weddingers, whom they wadna
thwart, sin' some o' theirsel's had made rinawa' marriages, wi' sma' credit if the truth
were told. Ony way, the Cambus Ha' family
took in the fugitives and gave them quarters
for the nicht. They cam' ower here the
next day to face the yerl, wha cursed and
blackguarded them ; but kennin' he could do
nae mair, though he lived to be a hunder,
suffered them to tak' the high road, while he
took the laigh.'

'I dare say he thought better of it, and
was reconciled to his daughter in the end,'
said Iris demurely; 'we are not so clever on
our side of the Borders as you are on yours,
Jeannie.'

* The celebration of marriages in private houses was
then almost universal in Scotland.

'So I hae heard say, mem. But the feck o' the couples were mair crafty than to let it be touch and go like that; whiles they would come dressed up sae as their ain mithers could hardly hae kenned them, or they would travel here by opposite roads and at different times. The bridegroom by hissel' or wi' a frien' would ride by a coach, and the bride would come, sometimes her lee-lane—eh! but she maun hae had a stout heart and a hantle faith in her lad—it micht be in the dead o' nicht, by anither.'

'And how did they do it, Jeannie? out of church, without a regular clergyman always. Did they never forget their prayer-books and the rings?' pressed Marianne, with the keenest curiosity.

'Prayer-books!' cried Jeannie, her trim figure, in its dark-stuff gown, white cap and apron, swelling at the very word. 'We haena had a service-book sin' auld Jenny Geddes flung her stule at the head o' the minister for dauring to pray in the kirk aff printed paper. As for the ring, it is but the bridegroom's giftie to the bride; it can be given at ony time. Na, we're no married wi' rings.'

'What are you married with then, in the name of wonder? Did you ever hear anything like it, Iris?' cried Marianne, as at an incredible but surpassingly ludicrous joke. 'I dare say you don't vow to love, honour, and obey your husbands, when you take them for better, for worse?'

'Na,' said Jeannie again, with a canny sense of humour, 'we say as little as we can, baith lads and lasses. Ye ken that least said is sunest mended. But there are waur husbands and wives than some you'll find in Scotland, mem.'

'I believe you,' said Marianne. 'I think you are a remarkable people, with charming institutions. If I ever marry, I'll come and do it in Scotland. But in order that I may know what I'm about, you must tell me what really takes place, what you can find to say, when it can be said, in so few words, either in a church or a house, or a "doocot," or wherever you may find yourselves.'

'Weel,' said Jeannie, slightly offended by the tone and the laughter, and defending herself with some dignity, 'we dinna believe that the Lord's confined to temples made wi' hands. We think the earth is His and the

fulness thereof, and that His een are open to
what's doing ower the whole world where
ilka place is His temple. When all is richt
and in order for a Scotch waddin', our minister
puts up a bit prayer out o's head, and there's
a sma' discoorse o' his own composition,'
Jeannie explained with emphasis, as if she
set great store on the originality of the performance. 'The discoorse may last for ten
or twenty minutes ; then there's another
prayer at the end. But the ceremony itsel'
which does the business needna tak' three
minutes.'

'Then what on earth does it consist of ?
It sounds exceedingly like the waving of a
magician's wand.'

'Na, there's nae magic aboot it. It's just
the speerin' and answerin' o' twa reasonable
questions. The minister, or it micht he
anither man in a rinawa' marriage, asks the
lad afore ane or twa witnesses, will he tak'
this woman to be his lawfu' wedded wife, and
he says " Yes," or he only boos if he's blate.
Syne the minister speers at the lass if she'll
tak' this man to be her lawfu' wedded husband, and she curtshies. Then the minister,
or the man ackin for him, says, " Join hands,"

49—2

and the twa cleek their fingers thegither. Neist the minister or the man proclaims, "What God has joined letna man put asunder;" and that's a', unless the signing o' the lines that certifies the fac'.'

'Do you mean to say you marry as an anonymous man and woman? Do you not even say "M" or "N"?' inquired Marianne, still full of interest and diversion.

'What's your wull, mem?' Jeannie questioned in her turn, using an ancient phrase which signified that she had not the most distant idea what her interrogator meant.

'It is not my will, it is yours, to marry in this odd mysterious fashion.'

'I beg your pardon, mem, but there can be nae mystery, or mockery either, about honest folk,' protested Jeannie indignantly. She felt strongly on such subjects as her nationality and her kirk, and had a settled conviction that she did well to be angry when they were attacked.

Iris interposed as a peace-maker.

'We only wished to know if you used no Christian name, such as Jeannie or Donald, in your marriage service.'

'Donald is a Hielant name,' said Jeannie

a little disdainfully. 'We hae nae Donalds among our Lowland Scotch—ony way none hereawa on the Borders. Na, we mention no names; at least we werena wont to bring them into the ceremony, though some new-fangled ministers say baith names, and would put it to me as Jean Maxwell, whether I would take Tam Riddel or Allan Elliot for my man?'

Apparently Jeannie had not the guile to use assumed names for her illustration, since she coloured violently, and added that she did not think the new fashion 'sae mannerly and modest' as the old. 'But there's the mistress's ring o' the bell. She'll say I've been claverin' instead of minding my wark, and deed she'll no be far wrang,' cried Jeannie in self-condemnation, as she caught up her broom and dust-pan and made a hasty retreat to the door, before Marianne could call after her:

'Say we kept you for the enlarging of our ideas. It is quite true, and she may put it in the bill.'

Marianne Dugdale was much struck and greatly enlivened by what she had heard of the runaway marriages, once of frequent occurrence in the house, and of the simplicity of the ceremony of marriage according to the Presbyterian Church of Scotland. She ran the two subjects together, and mixed them up inextricably in her mind, while she retailed the information she had got from the chambermaid, with great gratification, for the edification of the whole party. The topic was a promising one, full of sentimental interest, and yet fertile in jokes. Even the quietest and shyest person there, not to say the oldest, who was never behind with her joke, but as being a little of an invalid at present resigned herself to performing the part of a listener, could not resist expressing an opinion, and calling forth a laugh. But none was so full of the stories as Marianne Dugdale. Even after the girls had retired for the night she kept reminding Iris, ' what throbbing temples and beating hearts must have sought refuge in these rooms ! I wonder if no bride ever gave in at the last moment, fainted dead away, or said she would go back as she came, and try to be patient, and obey the law.'

' A runaway marriage was not breaking the law—the law of the land, I mean—that went with the couple,' said Iris. ' I think, like sensible Jeannie, that in extreme cases the remedy was open to trial. I have no doubt that the law existed for these, and to prevent weak women being hardly dealt with. It strikes me that there was a certain manliness and honesty in the law, though, of course, it might be much abused.'

'Of course,' echoed Marianne, without having paid much attention to what her companion had said. 'Don't you think it would be dreadful, horrible, to marry without love, Iris, even if the man were not a high-handed sinner, such as the girl described?'

Iris had never heard Marianne speak so seriously before, and even yet she was not sure that a jest might not lurk beneath the seriousness, till her cousin added in a tone of suppressed excitement :

'I would not do it for all the world ; I know it would be a terrible danger for me. It is another thing with you. I believe you would be good, and do your best under any circumstances. But I, Iris ; did it never strike you that there was something of— granny in me?' Marianne broke off and asked in a low tone with a slight shudder, but looking Iris full in the face all the time, as if to surprise her answer.

'No, no, nothing at all,' said Iris, startled and shocked, 'except that it goes without saying we are both of her blood, and in some physical points — features, tones of voice, tricks of gesture, we may bear a resemblance to her, as doubtless we do to each other,' added Iris, seeking to widen the chain of relationship to which she was referring.

'Ah, I know better,' said Marianne, drawing a long breath. 'I am hot-blooded, impulsive, headstrong, as she has been. I, too, could be brought to stand at bay, and to break through every obstacle in the path of my will. I know I am a weaker woman than she is, but sometimes I think it is not only because hers is the stronger nature, but because I am really like granny, that she can turn and twist and make a tool of me. I see perfectly well what she is about all the time, how she is touching every sensitive spot in my composition, stirring me up and egging me on to be vain, heartless, and treacherous. But I cannot resist her—I defy myself to do it. It is the same as bringing fire to tinder. I kindle up in a blaze in a moment, and become a puppet to be played off according to her pleasure. It is easy to guess what you will say, that I can strive, and watch, and pray to hold my own, but I am afraid I cannot. There is some sympathy between us. No, don't let us speak of it any longer, Iris, for even to allude to it in a whisper seems to make it a greater reality, and to render me more in her power.'

This impatient and, as it seemed, cowardly turning of Marianne's back on a cause for apprehension, with the avoidance of all present reflection and future resolution on the point, was a new practice to Iris Compton. She had faced each foe that stood in her path, whether or not she had been worsted in the contest.

But there was no room at this date for rational remonstrance with Marianne Dugdale. The moment her humour changed, which it was apt to do in the twinkling of an eye, she would put her small hands over her shell-like ears and call out pettishly she was not to be preached to, though she had just challenged and almost solicited the sermon. She would prefer to advance partially blind-

folded to threatened destruction, rather than
endure the sharp pain, acute self-reproach,
and mental trouble of opening her eyes,
counting the cost, and making a determined
stand and an abiding choice as to what was
to be her conduct and fate. At the same
time, poor little square-shouldered Marianne
was far less unstable by nature than from
defective training and untoward circumstances.

CHAPTER XXXV.

THE next morning rose with such a raw, white Scotch mist or drizzling rain as to catch everybody in the throat worse than her cold had caught Lady Fermor, and to forbid preliminary strolls and seats on the Border moors. The two young men tried them on several occasions, only to return thoroughly soaked, to be sent to the lower regions, where, as Marianne Dugdale declared, the pedestrians were turned before a slow fire: a process which afforded no comfort to the imprisoned ladies in the rooms above. Even in fine weather these moors are bleak in August, for the bloom of the broom is past, and the first purple of the heather is growing brown, before the burst of September red ling which lends the final glow to the wilderness. It was hard to be assailed

by the Scotch weather-fiend before the party
had done more than set foot in Scotland.

Marianne Dugdale was crusty when she
came down to breakfast in the inn parlour,
where Lady Fermor sent Soames to pour out
tea and play propriety at the table where the
young people gathered.

'Nobody shall say that I have not looked
after you.　After what I've seen and known,
I trust nobody,' the old lady told her nieces
insultingly.

'Very right, granny.　We've all heard
evil-doers are evil-dreaders,' retorted Marianne recklessly, while Iris crimsoned and
hurried out of hearing.

Marianne's temper was not improved by a
somewhat agitated announcement from King
Lud that he must leave them and start by
the night train.　He had not heard from the
Admiralty, but there were letters from the
Rectory, where he ought to have been weeks
before.　The mother had been ill; and even
without that obligation his last days on shore
were due to those at home.　They were too
kind to complain, but he should not have
failed them.

No, of course not.　Good little boys could

not play truant for any length of time, Marianne told him scornfully, while she crumbled
down the bit of oat-cake with which she had
provided herself, but could not eat, and eyed
superciliously the dish of newly caught trout.
But how anyone could leave his friends in
the lurch she could not understand, she went
on tartly. It would have been bad enough
to have deserted them before they had
reached their destination, but it was mean
to go in such weather.

He brightened up a little, and said earnestly : 'You must be aware I have no
choice, Miss Dugdale.' And then the big,
sandy-haired, full-faced lieutenant, the diver
among sharks and the defier of polar bears,
positively blushed like a girl, when he went
on : 'But I may comfort myself—may I
not ?—with the selfish hope that I shall be
missed—a little ?'

'Not unless by Iris or Lady Fermor or
Sir William,' Marianne assured him coolly.
'I never flatter a man's vanity. We can
really get on very well without you—can we
not, Sir William ?'

'If you like to put it so, Miss Dugdale,'
said Sir William a little awkwardly, and so

deliberately that Marianne could have shaken him, to have roused the man into greater alacrity. On second thoughts she decided that it would be a fine arrangement to force him to be on his mettle as her willing, engrossed servant for the day.

Ludovic Acton had deferred his departure till he should have to encounter the chill and darkness of midnight in such weather, in order—infatuated fellow—that he might have ten or twelve hours more to sun and scorch himself in the flame that was consuming him. Marianne proposed to repay him by rendering these hours one prolonged period of bitterness, till it was just possible the cruel cauterization of his wound might be complete and prove effectual, and the last boon be granted to him of departing limp and spiritless, but cured, if he were capable of cure, of a misplaced attachment to an unfeeling, ungrateful girl.

The prospect from the windows was not charming after the varied exercise and enjoyment of the past week. The bright red roses were shedding their petals, together with showers of tears, and were acquiring a cold purplish tinge in the process. The honeysuckle dangled and dripped depressingly. Nothing was to be seen beyond a few yards, except a white seething sea of vapour, which seemed to rise in huge puffs of steam as well as to fall down in rain. It had begun by swallowing up respectively every morsel of Skiddaw and Scafell, Criffell and the Lead Hills. Nothing remained save the mist itself.

It was a blank, disconsolate day for belated travellers at a country inn, a day to order a smoky fire to be lit, draw the scanty curtains, and aim at the severe discharge of duty, and the acquisition of a rampant sense of self-righteousness, by writing off a dozen letters —long due; to collapse into calling for refreshments, yawning and dawdling and telling idle stories ; to sour and ferment into quarrelling with might and main, and getting a little heat and vigour into life in that way.

Marianne tried none of these plans, for she did not deign to quarrel with King Lud ; it was not her cue to dispute with Sir William, except in spurts of uncontrollable exasperation ; she had a notion Iris would not wrangle with her, and Lady Fermor was not visible all the morning.

Marianne lugged Sir William into the passage to play battledore and shuttlecock by means of ancient implements for the game, which she had discovered in some corner, where they might have been kept in other years when the pastime was in the height of popular favour, and taken out on special occasions to divert the sorrows or fears of a childish bride, or to allay the restlessness of an excited bridegroom. But Marianne found that Sir William had to be taught, and though he insisted that he was good for rackets, he made no progress in catching and returning the mounted bunch of feathers. She sat down to backgammon with him, and found, to her disgust, that he could not only beat her to sticks, but did it without ceremony, with a wooden-headed adherence to the rules of the game, and a quiet grin of masculine superiority, which were beyond bearing. She rummaged out of her trunk silks and worsted, and set him to wind them for her, as Lady Thwaite had once done before. But either Sir William was now a more adroit master of the situation, or Marianne was not such an adept as Sir William's former employer in taking amuse-

ment out of her neighbour's blunders. Marianne asked her victim to read a guide-book
aloud while she worked ; but he read, accord·
ing to his custom, in a stentorian voice. so
that everybody in the room had the benefit
of the performance. It ceased to be private,
as she had intended, and the publicity did
not suit her, since she had a little weakness
for monopolizing men's notice—a weakness
which, with regard to Sir William Thwaite's
attentions this day, had become an urgent
necessity to her. In the end, between worry
and the noise her squire made in obeying her
last behest, her head began to ache violently.
Then it became evident that poor Marianne
was in a state of nervous weariness and
crossness, which, to her extreme mortification,
caused her to be viewed as an object of pity,
rather than of reprehension.

There was more sorrow than anger in King
Lud's kind eyes, and the sorrow smote Marianne Dugdale, so that she was barely able
to persist in the line of behaviour she had
adopted towards him and other people.
She was extremely offended by Iris's offer
of eau-de-cologne for her headache, the more
so, perhaps, that Iris had been conversing

for the last three-quarters of an hour, in the most natural, unaffected manner certainly, but still on confidential terms, with Ludovic Acton, on scraps of Rectory news and on his probable destination when he should get a ship. Iris had no right to such information as Marianne had not cared to seek. It was setting her at nought for King Lud to vouchsafe to an old friend—in Marianne's very hearing, too—the details she had declined to listen to. To sum up the sufferings of Marianne's dog-in-the-manger mood, she began to grow frightened at Sir William, whom she had only looked upon as a temporary servant to suit her purpose. She had raised up a spirit with which she could not cope, and that she did not understand. His looks and tones had changed to rueful, unbounded forbearance and repressed tenderness, as she had known them change on the morning at the Academy. Marianne could not comprehend it, and her ignorance abashed her for the moment in her perversity. Iris believed that his heart was melting and thrilling because he was thinking of his dead wife, poor, wild Honor, who had paid by her early, untimely death for all wherein she had offended him ; whom he had not made happy, save during the first few weeks of their short wedlock ; to whom, in the person of this capricious, captious, yet withal generous and warm-hearted girl, he might be called on in some sort to atone for his errors. What was he, or who cared for him, that he should decline to give up all that was left to him, in order that he might make the amends ?

And all the time Iris was as sure as she could be of the result of any human act, that if Sir William Thwaite were led on and suffered, by the contrivance of Lady Fermor and the folly of Marianne Dugdale, to accomplish the reparation which had more than once flashed across his mind, it would not only be a repetition of his former grievous blunder, it would be the consummation of the misfortunes of his chequered life.

Luncheon was welcome by way of variety, and still more dinner, with Lady Fermor declaring herself recruited in spite of the weather. She made no sign, if she observed the very visible dismemberment of the party, the discomposure of the individuals of whom it was composed, the heaviness, depression, and peevishness, as the effect of the rain, in

50—2

anticipation of the first break-up of the group
of friendly associates by the departure of
King Lud with the night train. Whether
Lady Fermor were cognizant of the tokens
or not, they did not augur a cheerful evening.

Appearances brightened, however, with
coffee. Lady Fermor was at her best, chatty,
with a rasping good-humour, inclined to
encourage the young people in any form of
diversion, though she still declared herself
unfit for her usual game of cards.

'But you boys and girls may set a-going
games for yourselves. What games we had
long ago, when we were not too wise or grand
or goody-goody to play games! Old-fashioned,
homely riddles and forfeits, when I was a
very small child, charades, tableaux, not to
speak of private theatricals for our own
benefit, without any shoddy pretence of helping charities or entertaining paupers. Why,
Marianne, are you so down in the mouth with
one day's rain that you cannot even get up a
sham penny reading?'

There had been a reaction from Marianne's
exhaustion before this speech, a return to the
restless excitement of the morning, deepened,
as in the case of all relapses. But it was

Lady Fermor's goad which sent the girl beyond all bounds of discretion and delicacy.

'Thank you, granny, for the suggestion, which I'll take leave to improve upon,' cried Marianne, with flaming cheeks and flashing eyes. 'Ladies and gentlemen, we shall act one of the runaway marriages, for which this place was once famous. It will be a play in a single scene, and the words are so few that nobody need pretend not to be equal to learning his or her part.'

'Bravo!' exclaimed Lady Fermor, with the baleful fires in her sunken eyes leaping up for an instant; 'if you are able to carry out the idea. But who will bell the cat? Who will assume the principal parts, and play bride and bridegroom?'

'"I, said the sparrow,"' quoted Marianne, with an assumption of sparrow-like pertness, 'I will play the bride, and I choose Sir William for my bridegroom.'

It was a bold speech, and seemed to take the person most concerned by storm.

'How am I to thank you for your condescension, Miss Dugdale?' he said, with an agitation and seriousness which were startling, and caused even Marianne to look put

out and to pause for a moment in her reck-
lessness.

'Oh, by acting as well as you can,' she said
hastily. 'I ask nothing further. I can coach
you; I can coach everybody. I heard all
about it from the maid. Somebody has to
ask the bride and bridegroom if "Barkis is
willin'?" and then we have only to say "yes"
or "boo," which seems to be letting us off by
an easier method than speaking—even in a
monosyllable. But what can "boo" mean?
I understand, and am able to say "bo" to a
goose'—with a fleeting, impatient glance at
King Lud, sitting back in a corner, with a
sudden lividness of cheek and lip, yet with
the self-control of a gentleman and an officer.
'But I confess "boo" beats me.'

'It means "nod," Marianne. Couldn't you
guess it by the corresponding word "curtshey"?' said Iris, speaking with an effort, as
if she were forcing herself to join in the conversation. 'But, if I were you, I would not
bow to such a bad jest. I think you might
find a better game.'

'Oh, we are too demure to go through
with a marriage even in a play,' said Lady
Fermor with suppressed rage, because her

opinion was disregarded. 'Or is it sour grapes, because the chief *rôles* are appropriated?'

'And the smallest and silliest of us can nod easily enough,' maintained Marianne, so that Iris was silenced.

Sir William glanced at her with a quick, disturbed inquiry; but he could not read her face or her heart.

'Acton'—Lady Fermor turned ruthlessly to the lieutenant—'you are glum enough to play the owl or the parson; you'll dig the grave—no, I did not mean that—you'll perform the ceremony.'

'Thanks, Lady Fermor'—he choked down his feelings—'but I am not qualified to take my father's place.'

'I'll teach you,' insisted Marianne flippantly; 'you have only to utter three simple sentences. You ask whether the man will take the woman and the woman the man for husband and wife; you bid them join hands, and then declare no power in heaven or on earth is ever to part them. Surely you can remember that.'

'Don't spoil sport, Acton,' enjoined Lady Fermor in her deep gutturals. 'We have no substitute, unless we call in the innkeeper—honest man ! as they say in his country—and he may not be able to see a joke.   You know you have to punch a hole in a Scotchman's head before you can get a joke into it. Never shirk what you've got to do, however much against the grain.   I thought that was part of a sailor's creed.'

'So it is,' said the badgered man, raising his head and pulling himself together.   'I'll do what you want.   Don't fear that I shall spoil sport, Miss Dugdale—Lady Fermor.'

'Are you all mad ?' implored Iris ; but she spoke in a low tone, and nobody, unless Sir William, heard her.

'Be off, Marianne,' urged Lady Fermor, entering into the spirit of the unseemly frolic, as she had entered into many another of the same description.   'It won't be hard for you to dress in character, since there are no white silks or satins, or veils or orange-blossoms, required here.   Your travelling-dress will do, and Thwaite need not change his coat. Your cousin Iris will not object to bring you in, and stay as a spectator, unless she holds that the bride's shoes are hers by prior right —is she so many months the senior or the junior of the two? I forget which—and ought not to be filled by other feet. I'll arrange where the men shall stand.'

Marianne went out of the room, with Iris following her sure enough ; but Iris did not overtake her cousin as she ran upstairs before the girl had passed Jeannie, the chamber-maid smilingly making room for her. The young lady had a roguish whisper for her humble ally.

'Jeannie, I'm coming down again to be married. The house has not lost its spell.'

'Eh ! Megsty me !' cried Jeannie, instinctively setting down the jug of hot water she was carrying for some gentleman's toddy, that she might not scald herself or any other person in the height of her excitement. But Miss Dugdale had already gone into her room, followed by the other young lady, looking 'that taken up' that she did not notice Jeannie.

In reality Iris was moved to the depths of her soul. The moment she was alone with her cousin Iris came out in a new character to Marianne. Iris went up to the little actress and poured forth, for her benefit, such a torrent of passionate upbraiding as the

gentlest lips will utter when the heart is
stirred with poignant sympathy, and the
honourable spirit outraged by what is unfair
and ungenerous, when the meekest man or
woman does well to be angry, and indignation
is only the expression of truth.

'How could you, Marianne Dugdale—how
could you have the heart? You may not
care for him a bit; but you see how he cares
for you, and if you had any pity, any womanly
feeling, you would spare him. It is only
acting, of course, and there might be no great
harm in that; but it is brutal—yes, brutal, to
get up such a farce, knowing what he is suffering. I cannot tell whether you are making
a fool of Sir William also; but you have no
right to do that either,' said Iris, holding up
her head, and flushing rosy red. 'He is a
man who, though he is not much older than
ourselves, has had great troubles and sorrows.
The knowledge of that alone should keep the
most thoughtless girl from harming him—
perhaps in a way she cannot guess, and yet
she may live to rue it. You are able to judge
for yourself that, like many a greater man, he
is simple and trustful in some things—where
women are concerned, for instance—in spite

of having had his eyes opened roughly already. That, too, should be his shield against hardened raillery and coquetry. You are free and right to choose for yourself, and if you and Sir William Thwaite choose each other nobody need object; all your friends must rejoice and wish you well. But to go trifling with Ludovic Acton, and torturing and shaming him at the last moment by this barbarous play, no good will come of it. I could never have believed it of you, Marianne.'

Iris ended, exhausted by her vehement defence of her friends and protest against wrong.

Marianne stared with big brown eyes, tried to laugh, turned away her head to hide her changing colour and drooping eyelids, and cried out ironically:

'Well, this is a tirade from a quiet-going young lady!' At last she sat down, crossed her arms, and faced her flushed, overcome accuser. 'So I don't care a straw for King Lud, and I have a sneaking kindness for Sir William, or rather for his place and title, I dare say. I am going to sell myself for a little rank and wealth, as thousands of girls

have done before me.   That is the way of it
—is it ?   Very creditable to me, and you
ought to know me by this time.   Never
mind.   Will you tell me just one thing, Iris ?
What business has Mr. Acton to go away
in such detestable weather, as if to face the
elements—in the rhetorical phrase—at their
very dismalest is a great deal better than a
comfortable enough inn with our company ?
He has no summons from the Admiralty,
compelling him to start on the instant ; he
has to get up a story of his mother's being ill
and wanting him, and it can't refuse it's
mamsie's lightest whim, pretty dear !'

'Oh, Marianne ! how can you be so horribly unreasonable and unkind !' Iris said
again with fresh wonder and wrath.   'It is
not why should Ludovic go, but why should
he have stayed so long, in consideration of the
little he has got for all he has given ?   He is
a good son and brother, however little you
may be capable of valuing such a character ;
and Mrs. Acton is a good mother, who
would not grudge her boy his happiness, or
make an outcry about her health for the purpose of recalling him.   You cannot imagine
how much he is thought of, how he is waited

and wearied for at the Rectory. And he is
going to sea, where there are special dangers
and deaths even for those who do not take
their lives in their hands and risk them, at
every opportunity, for their fellows, as our
King Lud has risked his. He may never
come back. I don't know that he cares at
this moment, which is your doing. Before he
knew you he had a happy and honourable
life before him, and he loves his people,
which you think to be rather a flaw in his
character. To-day may be the last time we
shall see him in this world—·dear old King
Lud! whom I have liked and respected, boy
and man. How I should mourn for him!
But how will you look, and what will you
say, if you are told next winter or next
summer that his ship has gone down to the
bottom of the sea, like the *Captain* and the
Eurydice and the *Atalanta*, and he has gone
down to the depths with it, or that he has
died far from home in some foreign hospital ?'

However she might look then, there could
be no question as to how she looked now;
she looked white as a sheet and trembled
like an aspen, and what she said was the

strange outbreak : 'Yet he will give his mother the last word, the last look, which ought to be mine.'

Then she put up her little hand to her face, and

'Like summer tempest burst the tears,'

with which the girl had been battling since morning. The storm was as short-lived as it was violent, and even while Iris looked on in dismay at the effect of her words, the big drops ceased to rattle down, the chest left off heaving with sobs, while Marianne began to accuse herself piteously, passionately, laughingly, for extremes are always meeting. 'I am a wretch of a girl, and he's the dearest, best of fellows, as gallant a man as ever stepped, as true as steel, as tender as only the best men can be. And what did you take me for, that you could think I preferred Sir William Thwaite, who has risen in the world, and been wild, and is reformed, and is well enough in his way ? But what drowning women did he save ? What shipwrecked crew did he rescue ? What torpedoes did he help to launch at the peril of his precious life — like — like Jove scattering thunder-bolts ?'

Iris looked up in sheer bewilderment at this extravagant laudation. She was tempted to put in the reservation : ' Where had he the opportunity, though he, too, fought and bled for his country ? And are there not spiritual conflicts and conquests harder and nobler by far than any physical warfare and victory ?' But she had not the chance, for it was Marianne's turn to speak, and she was making abundant use of the privilege.

' There is one good deed I have done him, I have saved him from the consequences of an unworthy choice,' she said, her voice, which had sounded shrilly eager and ex-ultant an instant before, suddenly sinking in despair.

' No, Marianne. He does not think so ; he never will. I have known him since we were children. I know how hard it is to offend Ludovic Acton ; how lenient he is to offenders ; how sure to forgive,' represented Iris earnestly.

' Yes, he will think he has made a fortu-nate escape after to-day,' persisted Marianne dolefully. ' No man could bear what he has had to bear and forget it.'

' But you mean to make it up with him

before he goes ? You won't go on now with this stupid, coarse play, surely, surely, Marianne ?' besought Iris.

Marianne shook her head in wilful determination to suffer the worst penalty she had brought upon herself, and with a perverse doggedness which was characteristic of the girl : ' I cannot ; it is too late. It would make no difference now. Besides, we are not on terms to admit of an explanation, and I dare say he will be thankful in years to come that there never has been the ghost of an engagement, or even of a mutual understanding between us,' she said sadly. ' I would not let him speak, or grant him the least satisfaction. I did not wish to bring the game to an end by allowing him to commit himself, and by being forced to commit myself either way. It was a game in the beginning, though it has ended in earnest. Oh dear ! I liked it so much while it lasted—to feel my power, and know I could make everything bright or dark to him by a word, a look. It was dreadfully inconsiderate and selfish to him, no doubt, and I shall be punished as I deserve.'

Iris was altogether taken aback, though

she had not been without her suspicions, but she knew Marianne Dudgale too well to protest :

'How could you have been so silly, so perverse, as to plague and grieve and do all you could to alienate the man you really cared for all the time ? How could you seek to attract another man, and seem as if you, in your turn, were attracted by him, when, during your whole acquaintance, you were perfectly indifferent—in that way—to his merits and to all that was pathetic in his history ?'

Where would have been the use in saying so, when Iris believed it had been, and might still be, quite possible that Marianne Dugdale, with the secret, violent fancy she had grown to entertain for the young fellow she had been domineering over and tantalizing, would consent, in a fit of pique and spleen, or mere sudden collapse and surrender to Lady Fermor's evil influence, to marry the other man, for whom she had no fancy, and who had little better to offer her than a second-hand, remorseful pity?

What Iris did say was the evident truth, that Marianne would punish at least one

other person as well as herself, the innocent
with the guilty.   And Iris pled :

'Won't you say, or let me say, that you
have thought better of it, and cannot carry
out this absurd, unbecoming mimicry of a
marriage ?   That will be some compensation
to Ludovic before he goes, and he may understand—may suspect.'

'No, no,' cried Marianne, starting up in a
fresh access of wilfulness and waywardness,
'I am not going to crave mercy from any
man, or seek to call him back.   Besides, I
am certain that granny would begin to jeer
and taunt me till I became possessed, and
then my last error would be worse than my
first.   Let us act the marriage and have
done with the whole thing.   I believe he has
renounced me already in his heart ; let him
have the comfort—the sop to his pride, poor
fellow—of doing it in so many words.   The
circumstance that he can speak them before
us all is a testimony which he may hug to the
end of his days, because it will prove how
fully he recovered from his delusion in time.
After I have treated him as I have done, and
gone so far, I owe him his revenge, and do
you think I'll stint him in it ?'

Marianne, in perfect sincerity, doubled in the argument, and twisted it round to make herself and everybody miserable in an ingenious fashion of her own, which is yet not altogether uncommon.

In any imminent danger in which Iris had ever seen a fellow-creature, her immediate strong instinct had always been to save the threatened victim—to save at Iris's expense, if need were—as when the girl controlled her natural recoil and held close the severed artery in her servant's wrist, as when she walked back to Whitehills with Lady Thwaite, dressed in a groom's clothes, and faced a man whom she had reason to know she had deeply offended, and whom all her friends and neighbours were then denouncing as a drunken ruffian. The instinct did not fail to assert itself at this juncture.

'Let me act the bride,' she said with quiet determination. 'It will be all the same who takes the part in a piece of child's play that neither Sir William nor I need mind, and it will save you and Ludovic Acton from a last misunderstanding, which, though it is only about a silly joke, may separate you for life.'

51—2

Marianne hesitated, with changing colour and parted lips. Her susceptible pride and fiery temper had been up in arms a moment before. She had forbidden a compromise, yet she might snatch at a reprieve. Her decision would be very much a matter of chance, as were many of the resolutions she formed in her honest but unregulated mind— even when they were on subjects of vital importance to her—taken on the spur of the moment, at haphazard, and under the influence of trifles light as air.

In the meantime Iris, awaiting Marianne's answer, frightened to look at her for fear of influencing her, looking on the floor instead, was calling King Lud her brother in her heart, and remembering all that his family had done for her—Iris Compton. She was thinking of Marianne's affectionate championship soon after they had become acquainted, and what a different world it had been to a lonely girl when she had found a bright, frank, young companion, generous and lovable even in her transparent follies, constantly by her side. Iris was thinking of Sir William and the debt he had already paid to Lady Fermor, and the other debt he had paid to

Honor. Iris's mind was even recurring to old stories and old wrongs in which her ancestor had been the wrong-doer and Marianne Dugdale's the sufferer of the wrong.

'What an excellent idea!' cried Marianne suddenly. 'You can play the bride, as you say, as well as I. They will not suppose that I have drawn back—only that we have agreed to change places. Indeed, as our hats and travelling-dresses are alike, and the light is none of the best, if we had not been so different in height, they might not have known the one from the other,' she ended with a little uncertain laugh, beginning to recover her courage and spirits. 'I wonder if he will give a great start and gape, forget all I told him, and not be able to proceed with the ceremony? Won't he look dreadfully foolish? But I shall not have vexed him— the very last thing. Iris, it was taking a despicable advantage of me to work upon my feelings and pretend he would not come back safe and sound—a great, strong, fearless fellow like King Lud, twice as big as our boys at home, with a face like a full moon. Yes, indeed, it is true; but I hate small faces in men; I think they cannot be too big every way. He has so often gone away, and always returned like a bad halfpenny. I wonder how and when we shall meet next,' melting into tenderness, but rushing off at a tangent the next moment. 'He can never be so base as to forget "the girl he left behind him." Remember, I shall be fit to kill you if he should jilt me, after what you have made me tell you. In the meantime I'll play that tune, in my own honour, every day that I can reach a piano, till he come back. Must he stay away months? A whole year or more? The man should not have made me so accustomed to his tiresome ways. How will the time pass without them? Shall I grow sick with hope deferred? And do all the girls in my position complain of the cruelty of the Queen and the Lord High Admiral? Who would have said I should be a spoon? How our boys would laugh, and even Cathie and Chattie would giggle. But they shan't know a syllable till he is a captain, and able to propose for me to granny or papa in due form. I suppose that will not be till he has made a pot of money, poor fellow, to keep me with; but, if the ruling powers continue long obdurate, we'll know what to do ; we'll run straight away to Scotland. Then we'll have to go into sea-side lodgings, and be careful of our coals, and never allow ourselves an extra pair of boots. Will you still acknowledge us, Iris ? You ought to, for you have been at the bottom of the mischief—even though granny has nothing more to say to us. By the way, we must not keep her waiting any longer. She will not stand the further delay of this marriage.'

Iris was hardly listening now as they proceeded to put on their travelling jackets and hats of brown tweed, with which they had provided themselves in preparation for what they had been pleased to consider the Arctic climate of Scotland.

'What a dress for a bride!' cried Marianne, in lively disgust.

'But it is a runaway bride,' said Iris.

'Yes, but depend upon it if she ran away of her own accord, she had some respect for her own feelings and those of her bridegroom, and put a bridal touch somewhere to her dress. Besides, my dear child, there must be something to mark the difference between us—in our parts. Here, take this bunch of wet roses—I dare say they are the descendants of bridal roses—which Jeannie brought me from the kailyard. Roses are later in the north than in the south; we are not travelled girls, so we may speak of Scotland and England—all we know—as north and south. Fasten the flowers in your jacket.'

Iris did as she was bidden to please Marianne, and, get the sooner done with the foolish play. The couple hurried downstairs arm-in-arm, and entered the room so abruptly that it was not difficult to picture an angry father at their back.

Somebody had drawn a table before the corner where Ludovic sat, looking grim. Sir William was standing beside it with a curious mixture of affront—as if doing something preposterous—and wistful yearning and pain in his face.

Lady Fermor sat still in the chair which she had before occupied, but she must have rung for Soames in order to enable her maid to enjoy the little entertainment, for the long lank functionary was ranged behind her mistress's chair.

The room was dark from the state of the

weather and the old-fashioned little windows;
besides, the company were not quick enough
to take up at once the cue of the roses with
which Marianne had obligingly supplied
them. Iris had volunteered to act her part,
and was doing what she needed to do with a
growing reluctance which became so nearly
insupportable that she could not stop to
think what she was about, but must hasten
through it, behaving like a creature in a
dream.

Marianne took the initiative, as she was
always disposed to do. She walked straight
up to Sir William. There she paused for a
second. In truth, she was not at all clear
how the office of giving away a runaway
bride was performed in the strange Scotch
marriage. She was afraid Jeannie had forgotten something. Marianne had to use her
own judgment; she wisely confined herself
to dumb show. She simply dropped Iris's
arm and retreated, leaving her cousin standing
by Sir William.

King Lud leant forward confounded, yet
eager as at an unlooked-for release from a
piece of sport which had galled him like a
wanton insult, a real irreparable injury.

Lady Fermor put up her hand to her eyes, as if to clear her sight, and let it fall again, sitting upright, with her eyes glittering, and nodding her head, as if she were the person called upon to bow her consent.

Sir William flushed scarlet, and looked, like a man driven wild, from one to the other. He could read nothing in Iris's little face; it was blank, like that of one forcing herself to stifle every warring inclination and go on with an ordeal.

'Proceed with the marriage, Mr. Acton; there is the bride,' muttered Marianne *ex officio*, with a little quiver, partly of laughter, partly of another feeling, in her voice.

Ludovic Acton started up to obey his mistress's behest, while life was once more opening out before him with hope and love and joy among its possibilities. Why had he been such a fool? How could he have been so taken in, to torture himself as he had done? This acting a marriage was nothing, the merest jest, when Marianne Dugdale was not to play the bride to another bridegroom than himself. It was no worse than fifty charades and *tableaux vivants*, in which he had taken part. If it had been so,

Iris Compton, good little Iris, whom he knew so well and could depend on entirely, would not have been in it. He stood behind the table facing Sir William and Iris, and tried to respond to Marianne's appeal, and to do credit to what she had told him when he had utterly mistaken her intention. He looked imploringly at her for inspiration, instead of at the pair before him. He sought to recall the sentences she had repeated to him. If he made a verbal mistake it would be forgiven in an actor who had only once heard his part.

'Will you take this woman for your wife?'

Marianne, who had drawn nearer the couple, turned prompter again—this time on behalf of Sir William—with the pantomime of an emphatic nod ; but he took them all by surprise, speaking out distinctly and so loudly as to sound roughly, 'I will.'

'Will you take this man for your husband?'

'Boo, or "curtshey," Iris,' whispered Marianne mischievously. Iris smiled slightly, as at a dimly apprehended, far away bit of fun, and inclined her head.

The impromptu parson looked despairingly at Marianne, who in answering despair

clasped her hands, shaking her head reproachfully at the same time.

'Join hands,' cried Ludovic.

Sir William put out his hand and grasped
Iris's in so tight a clasp that it half roused
her. She made a little motion to draw her
crushed fingers away. He was the better
actor of the two certainly, but he overacted
his part. Iris was so far recalled to herself
that she became aware of a stir at the room
door. Glancing in that direction she saw, to
her vague distress, it had been left open and
pushed slightly ajar, and that there was quite
a group of people on the threshold, the most
of them seeking to see without being seen.
Jeannie, the chambermaid, formed one bash-
ful spectatress; another gazer was the landlord, a thick-set, shock-headed man, who still
wore mine host's conventional red waistcoat.
But he was not skulking, whatever his companions might be; he held a candlestick with
a lit candle in his hand, for the rainy gloaming was fast deepening into mirk. He
looked excited, as if he wanted to come in
and either interfere with the performance or
join in it.

Apparently Lady Fermor had also detected

the intruders, for she called out, 'There, that will do!' and sure enough the group melted and vanished, pulling the door close behind them. But her ladyship, who was in high glee, might not so much intend to give a reprimand as to say the scene had been sufficiently represented; for she added immediately afterwards, addressing her own party, 'We need not mind signing the register or the bride's "lines." Upon my word, it has been a very pretty wedding. Let me congratulate you, Thwaite and Iris—that is my part of the performance, and a very pleasant part it is, I can tell you. You have given us a good notion of what a runaway marriage is like. I suppose, Iris, you thought, after all, you were the fittest match for the bridegroom.'

The hands so lately joined had already dropped asunder. Sir William remained standing alone by the table, as if he were trying to reason with himself, to get rid of a momentary hallucination, to cast off a disordering, maddening impression. He did not go near Lady Fermor. He hardly suffered himself to throw a look after Iris as she rejoined Marianne.

'How stupid you were, Mr. Acton,' Marianne accused King Lud. 'It was I, not you
who married them. I must ask Jeannie if
that is correct, and if a woman can marry a
couple in this improper little Scotland.'

Iris left the room with Marianne to put off
their out-of-doors habiliments. As the girls
did so, the roses fell unheeded from Iris's
jacket on the floor, and would have lain there
to be trampled under foot if Sir William had
not stepped forward, stooped, and picked
them up.

When the cousins came back, the subject
of the acted marriage was dropped as if by
common consent. The talk had turned upon
the lieutenant's departure, the hour for which
was drawing near. He had engaged a trap
from the innkeeper to take him through the
rain and darkness to the nearest station, a
few miles off. He was far brighter and more
animated than he had been all the day, while
Marianne Dugdale, on the contrary, became
somewhat silent, only emitting an occasional
little jet of contradiction and sauciness. He
announced confidently that he expected to
see them all again before he sailed, and
nobody deprived him of the hope, and forbade

him the privilege. If he wrung Marianne's
hand in saying good-bye, nobody could see
and censure the deed, since she did not
wrench her fingers away; for that matter
she had not flouted him for the last five
minutes, but if she cried herself to sleep and
bemoaned her former perversity and cruelty,
it was in the silence and solitude of her
room.

Iris thought it was charity to everybody
to adopt Lady Fermor's early hours this
night. A sudden sobriety which was almost
oppressive, the natural result of contending
emotions and of King Lud's going, had
fallen upon the young people. As for herself,
she desired nothing better than to be able to
recall undisturbed the whole events of the
day, including the grotesque farce in which
she had been involved. When she had
thought it all over, she would dismiss it from
her mind at once and for ever.

The dismissal was not quite so easy as Iris
had anticipated. She felt haunted by the
foolish play; she tossed on her bed sleepless
and feverish. When she did drop asleep,
she dreamt she had married Sir William
Thwaite in earnest without intending it; and

what was worse, she had not asked his leave, and he had not spoken one word or given a single glance, in renewal of his passionate love-making and proposal to her in the hay-field at Whitehills four years before. Nay, he had seemed at every crisis to turn—with whatever mixed motives—to Marianne Dugdale.

At last Iris slept soundly ; but even then she was disturbed by the business of the inn, or by the figments of her own imagination. She thought she heard some one calling her name loudly and urgently, and when she started up in bed and listened and failed to distinguish a voice speaking to her, she seemed to hear the noise of wheels driving rapidly from the door.

CHAPTER XXXVI.

THE BEAST RISES UP A PRINCE.

Iris slept late after a troubled night, and when she awoke and looked at her watch she could take nothing into account save that she had been shockingly lazy, though the sun was shining brightly enough after the rain to tempt all exemplary travellers to be up and abroad on unfamiliar ground. Iris grudged losing the bright morning, and she grudged still more keeping Marianne Dugdale, Sir William Thwaite, and Soames hanging about till she should choose to appear for breakfast. She had no time to spare for more than the general confusion with which the incidents of the past day—especially if they have been of an unusual character and crowded together —are apt to present themselves to people on their first awakening from a few hours' welcome oblivion.

Iris for once took refuge in self-evasion, for she had a half-formed notion, after her dim, partly remembered dreams, that she too had acted rashly and foolishly in what had passed, though it was no more than in being guilty of an appearance of evil in yielding to figure in an indiscreet, not too delicate parody of a solemn service. She might well feel provoked and mortified by discovering that she had put herself, unless her companions were considerate and forbearing—and when had Lady Fermor been either the one or the other?—in an awkward, embarrassing position? It was not to be thought that nobody—Marianne in her thoughtlessness, Lady Fermor in her malice, even Sir William in some blundering fashion—would ever allude to the rainy day at the inn on the Borders, and the amusement to which the party had resorted in order to spur on the lagging hours. If such allusions were made, how was Iris to look; what was she—or, when it came to that, what was Sir William —to think?

When Iris ran downstairs, half unwilling to face her companions, and yet eager to have the meeting over, she believed she

was later than she had suspected. The maid
Jeannie, standing at one of the doors on
the landing, withdrew into the room as if
ashamed for Iris's credit to encounter her at
such an hour, and unwilling to detain her,
while another servant, Iris fancied, looked at
her with tittering significance.

But what was Iris's surprise when she
entered the inn parlour and found it empty,
with breakfast only laid for one ! She rang
the bell in a little trepidation, for she was
conscious that Marianne was capable of playing her a trick, though Iris considered it
would be especially unkind and undeserved
this morning.

As another instance of the unexpected
happening, the landlord chose to wait in
person, bringing in the dish of trouts as his
excuse for his presence. 'Where are the
others ?' Iris inquired, without waiting for
the departure of the single rustic young
waiter, who was also favouring her with
his attentions, and showing no hurry in
depositing and arranging the tea and coffee
service so as to satisfy a scrupulous taste.
'Have they all breakfasted and gone out ?
I am afraid I am very late ;' and Iris tried

52—2

to smile instead of feeling absurdly discon-
certed.

The landlord did not hasten to answer her
with civil fluency. He began staring at her
in silence. 'Do you not know, miss, they
are gone?' he said at last, cautiously.

'Gone!' exclaimed Iris, not able to believe her ears. 'Ah! for a morning's excursion, I suppose,' she took heart to exclaim.
'But Lady Fermor never drives out before
luncheon, and Mrs. Soames cannot have left
her.'

'The leddy and her maid and the other
young leddy went first,' said the landlord
with precision. 'The gentleman only left
about an hour syne.'

'An hour ago?—that was still early. What
could influence Lady Fermor to go out even
earlier? Where have they gone? When
are they coming back?' cried Iris, in unre-
strained bewilderment.

'That I cannot take it upon me to say,
miss—you should know better than me.
But I apprehend you're in error on one point.
You seem to think all your party went the
same gate, nigh hand together?'

Iris nodded, her tongue refused its office.

The man looked a respectable man, and was
respectful enough in his manner, but the
wariness with which he conducted the conversation was remarkable, and there was in
his tone the slightest shade of irony not un-
mixed with dry humour—if she could have
recognised it—and a degree of perplexity. It
was as if he suspected her—while he was
haunted by a doubt—of still playing a part,
and had no objection to let her see he suspected her.

'Now, you're wrang there, begging your
pardon. First there was the young gentleman who took the trap to catch the last train
overnight, but I think you were with the four
when he set out. Syne, not long past the
sma' hours, between four and five o'clock,
when the rain was still spittin', afore the inn
was richt astir, the auld leddy sent for me
and but to be aff to meet the first train,
though it was a fell-like fatigue for a woman
at her time of life. Her body-woman was
dressed and ready like her mistress, but the
young leddy seemed laither to quit her pilly.
She did not come down till the chaise was at
the door, and then she made such a colly-
shangie calling out for somebody after she

was in the carriage, and wanting to stop and go back, that she was like to wauken the whole house.   But the auld leddy maistered the lassie—that I should speak so unmannerly—and drove off in spite of her.   Lastly,' and mine host looked still more curiously at Iris from under his eyebrows, ' there was the titled gentleman, who did not appear to have been disturbed any more than yourself, miss, for he just came quietly down at his usual hour.   It was only after he found that so many of the party were gone that he wrote a letter or two in haste—sending off one by a messenger—asked for a time-table, and left to meet the mid-day train. He did not speak to me of coming back when he paid his share of the bill—what was left after the auld leddy cleared the score—though he may have mentioned it otherwise, as it is what one would expect,' the speaker observed meditatively. ' However, he left a bit parcel for you in my hands,' the innkeeper went on briskly, as if the truth might lie in this nutshell, extracting a small packet from his waistcoat-pocket and placing it ostentatiously before Iris ; ' and it need be no secret that it was he wrat one of the letters which were left for you that I jalouse you have not seen.' He bustled to bring two letters from where they were stuck conspicuously in a card-rack on the chimney-piece, and laying them on her plate, left her at last with evident reluctance and disappointment at her reticence. In any other circumstances Iris would have been amused by the worthy man's inquisitiveness, and by the mingled shrewdness and simplicity with which he betrayed that he had been speculating on her affairs, and putting two and two together in order to bring out the sum of them to his satisfaction. But she was far past such amusement. She sat for a moment before opening the letters, staring at them mechanically with a stunned sensation. The one was in her grandmother's big, blurred, shaken handwriting; the other displayed the square upright characters which Sir William Thwaite's pen was wont to produce.

Iris tore open her grandmother's letter first. It contained only a few lines:

' DEAR IRIS,

'I am glad you have come to your senses at last, though I must own you took

me—and I presume more than me—by surprise.   However, when that person was perfectly agreeable, there is no more to be said.
All's well that ends well.   As I think you
and Sir William had better be left to yourselves like other young fools, for your honey-
moon, I have taken myself and Marianne
Dugdale off with the greatest expedition.
You ought to give me credit for my youthful
activity.   I trust to see you whenever you go
to Whitehills, and I have returned to Lambford.

' I remain your affectionate grandmother,
'MARIANNE FERMOR.

' P.S.—As Scotch marriages properly at-
tested, which yours can easily be, are quite
legal, if I were you and Thwaite I should
not put myself to the trouble and expense
of a re-marriage with the benefit of clergy,
favours, and cake, and a crowd of idle onlookers.   In fact, these re-marriages are often
great mistakes, mere sources of confusion and
misconception; so the less you have to do
with them, in my opinion, the better; but
please yourselves.

'M. F.'

Here at least were basest betrayal and desertion; whether premeditated or the instant relentless improvement of an unfortunate opportunity for gaining an end and paying back the opposition to an imperious will, Iris could not tell, then or ever. She thrust back the paper with trembling fingers into the envelope. As she turned it over she first looked beyond the handwriting, and read the address. It was to—

'*Lady Thwaite,*
Of Whitehills.'

She flung down the letter as if it stung her. While she did so a vision of Honor, who had last borne the title, rose before her. Poor Honor, who had so scandalized the public, had she ever acted more imprudently, or felt so degraded and disgraced as Iris did upon this miserable morning?

Iris read the address of the other letter before she opened it, and it gave her a grain of comfort, for it bore the familiar direction to Miss Compton.

'MADAM,' Sir William must have written first in his massive letters, then he had

squeezed in ' Dear ' at the edge, as if conscious, on reading over the note, that he
was warranted, nay, bound in exchange of
confidence, to use the friendly prefix in cold
blood,—' I am confounded by Lady Fermor's
unexpected departure. I feel that she has
taken a gross advantage of you, by repre-
senting in another light what I can never
presume to regard as anything more than
your having been induced to lend your
countenance to a frolic of Miss Dugdale's.
Perhaps Lady Fermor means this last act
as something of the same kind; but a
frolic which I am sorely afraid must incon-
venience and distress you for the time, is too
much of a good thing. I have come to the
conclusion that the best I can do for your
relief is not to stay here a moment longer.
I will go away instantly and await your pleasure elsewhere. Perhaps I had better stop
at Dumfries, in place of following Lady Fermor to Moffat. It sounds too much that
you should wish to write to me, but if it is
necessary, I shall get the letter at the post-
office there. You have done so much for
me and mine in the past, that I think you
will do me the justice of believing that I

would die rather than vex you—far less
intrude upon and insult you.

'Your obedient servant,

'WILLIAM THWAITE.'

Here was no treachery, and if she were
forsaken the deed was done out of manly,
grateful, jealous care for her best interests—
as a faithful brother would shield his sister.
It was clear that the letter had been written
in agitation and with anxious pains, no less
than with earnestness of purpose. The strong
characters had not faltered; but there were
erasures, as if he had found difficulty in
expressing himself.

Iris was both comforted and troubled by
the letter—comforted that her old friend, as
she had come to consider him, was not
destined to fall lamentably in her estimation
by becoming her deadliest foe. On the contrary, he was as innocent as herself, and he
was judging wisely and acting truly in the
painful dilemma into which they were both
brought by Lady Fermor's wicked will and
their own weakness. The foolish trouble
which darkened this ray of comfort was for
the most part a selfish, vain trouble, as Iris

told herself with some bitterness.   Still, however inconsistent, she could not help wasting
a regret on the complete dispelling of old
associations, the conviction of the utter ex-
tinction of his early feelings for her.   His
love had not appeared wise or suitable, or
even seemly to her—nobody had felt that
more strongly than she herself had felt it in
those days.   Still the knowledge of the
destruction, root and branch, of the old
desperate regard, cost her a pang.   More-
over, it would be grievous for him if he had
learnt to love, too late and in vain, Marianne
Dugdale, on whose share in the recent cruel
proceeding he had not cast a shadow of
blame.

But there was another communication from
Sir William besides the letter, which he had
possibly intended to be all, till something had
occurred to him at the last moment that had
caused him to turn, make up the packet, and
entrust it to the landlord.   When Iris un-
fastened the paper she stared at the contents
stupidly for a moment, while her colour went
and came in mute amazed protest.   He had
enclosed two ten-pound notes—probably the
greater part of the money he had about him

—in a cover, on which he had written in pencil : ' Will you do me the honour to accept this loan in case you should want it ?'

' In case she should want it !' as she read the sentence, she realized the truth fully for the first time. She had been left behind, abandoned in what the people of the house might well view as compromising circumstances, a young woman alone in a strange inn, on the borders of a strange country. And whether she should determine to follow her grandmother, upbraid her with her barbarity and insist on her undoing her part of the play ; or whether she should attempt the return journey by herself over more than half the length of England to seek the protection of Mrs. Haigh ; or to throw herself on the old friendship of the Actons at the Rectory—her slender purse would have been unequal to the demands either of the shorter or the longer expedition, since Marianne Dugdale, having spent her own quarter's salary, had freely borrowed from Iris. She would have been without the means of paying her expenses in any direction had it not been for the humanity of Sir William Thwaite.

Iris felt humbled and distracted, unable to

fix what she should do, yet aware that she
must do something without loss of time. She
tried to swallow her breakfast as the first
necessary task to be performed. Then she,
too, studied the time-bill, but shrank uncon-
querably from the possibility of encountering
Sir William at the little wayside station.
The landlord had spoken of the mid-day train;
apparently not many trains stopped at this
out-of-the-way junction, and he might not
be gone by the time she reached the place.

As she began to recover from the blow
and her natural presence of mind and power
of resource returned to her, it struck her that
the obviously sensible course for her to pur-
sue was to stay where she was, till she had
contradicted to the people of the house the
false impression they had received. Some of
them, from whatever cause, had been witnesses to the carrying out of the ill-timed
jest—in keeping with the old reputation of
the house. The natives of the place were
well acquainted with this reputation, in which
they took a shamefaced pride. The misconception of the inhabitants was deepened
by their knowledge that irregular, but at the
same time lawful, marriages could still be

performed within their precincts, as for that
matter within the entire bounds of Scotland.
Above all, their credulity was imposed upon
by the coarsely cruel conduct of Lady Fermor.

As Iris reflected, her courage and even
her spirits, though they had been greatly
tried, revived a little. In spite of the outrageous interpretation which Lady Fermor
had chosen to put upon the story, it was
simply preposterous. Nobody could treat it
seriously for a moment. Neither the pretended bride nor bridegroom was in earnest,
and as little was King Lud who spoke the
words, or Marianne Dugdale who prompted
them. She was at the bottom of the practical
joke, and yet she had strangely, though not
without protest, according to the innkeeper,
gone over to the enemy. Of course no
reasonable person could attach the slightest
importance to the scandal.

Iris did not suffer her heart to fall before
the disheartening recollection of the limited
number of reasonable persons in the world,
and the sorrowful comprehension that the
bare breath of the most incredible scandal is
baleful, even where the sins of the fathers
are not visited on the children.

CHAPTER XXXVII.

THE LAW OF THE LAND.

THE landlord had appeared to lay himself
out for Iris's confidence, but he had not
uttered his suspicions in so many words. Iris
had not inherited her grandmother's pro-
pensity of invariably choosing men for her
advisers. It would be doubly disagreeable
for Iris to try to make a man measure the
extent of the late piece of folly—as mere
folly. Yet she wanted a mouth-piece to tell
it to all who would listen. Her security lay
in the immediate publication of the truth,
and her inclination pointed to the bright yet
douce girl Jeannie, who had spoken only too
graphically and amusingly of the Border
marriages to the English young ladies.

Iris, walking restlessly about the room, saw
from the end window Jeannie, in her morning
calicot wrapper, linen apron and bare arms,

carrying a great basketful of wrung-out clothes to spread over a washing-green. Iris took a swift resolve to go out and talk to the girl and tell her the truth, which she would surely convey to her master and mistress.

As Iris traversed the rambling passages of the old house and sought the way to the washing-green, she was oppressed by the consciousness of having become the centre of attraction to her neighbours, while they openly or covertly looked at and watched her. This knowledge when it mingles in any transaction of life, whether joyful or sorrowful, lends a strange unreality to the affair, and gives to the performers in the true drama a double sense of being at once the veritable persons who are passing through a glad or miserable crisis in their history, and at the same time actors on a stage, playing, whether they will or not, for the benefit of onlookers.

Iris found Jeannie busily employed on a haugh or strip of meadow by the side of one of those rapid, white and brown, brawling streamlets, 'the bonnie burnies,' with their endless songs, which are among the chief delights of the North country. Though the brook was swollen by the rains of yesterday, so that every slippery stepping-stone was covered, and its clear water rendered turbid, yet it did its best to flash in the sunshine and 'jouk' round each corner.

Jeannie glanced up from her occupation and made one of the 'curtsheys,' which, unless in remote country places, and among very primitive people, form now the depth of respectful greeting reserved solely for royalty.

Iris had grown nervous, or else Jeannie was really shyer than she had been before, and the single look which she gave was not directed so much to the visitor's face, as to her uncovered left hand. Was Jeannie looking in vain for that 'bit giftie' of a wedding-ring, which, though it plays no part in the Scotch marriage ceremony, is always bestowed as the first token from the husband to the wife, and in this light is regarded as a proof of marriage and universally worn, till death, in Scotland as well as in England?

'Oh! what a miserable day it was yesterday, Jeannie!' began Iris, referring to the weather.

'Did you think sae, my leddy?' inquired

Jeannie, as if there could be two opinions on
the subject, while she completed laying out
a row of towels on the grass.

'Did you not think so? Have you so
much worse weather?' Then Iris added
hastily, with regard to the changed form of
address which Jeannie had used, that had
struck the listener's roused ear, ' But I'm
not "my lady"; only my grandmother, the
old lady who left early this morning, is
entitled to be spoken to in that way.'

'As you like, mem,' said Jeannie slowly
and doubtfully. 'You should ken best; it is
for you to tak' your choice how you're to be
ca'd. For the weather, weel, whiles we've
deep snaw in the winter, and sleet as late as
April, and rain—no' drizzlin' but poorin' in
buckets-fu', with spates in the burn till it
rins ower a' the haugh, and the beasts are
flooded in the byre and the stable, and we're
keepit in the hoose for twa or three days at a
time. But I was meaning that it is often
the mind that makes the weather to folk;
the sun will be shinin' for some when there's
nocht but cluds for others—div you no think
sae, mem? In that case yesterday michtna
hae been sae dowie a day to you.'

Jeannie, in spite of her momentary bashfulness, was not unwilling to approach the subject Iris wished to discuss. In fact, the girl was dying to pick up some crumbs of information if the young lady would drop them. The whole house was on the alert in reference to the supposed marriage which had taken place, and in addition to Jeannie's craving for a share in an exceptional and half-forbidden experience, the friendly heart pitied ' the bonnie young leddy, left her leelane the day after her marriage, by her very man.' This was the great and not to be admired eccentricity in the proceedings, which more than the failure to summon Long Fernie or a substitute to tie the knot, and so keeping the business strictly among the party themselves, had puzzled and exercised the minds of the inn household, and of such boarders and customers as were privileged to be privately informed of the occurrence. It was not unusual for the bride or the bridegroom expectant to make their entrances on the scene separately, as Jeannie had told Iris and Marianne, but it had been the good old custom that they should make their exit in company.

'Yesterday was dowie, if that means un-happy, to me, Jeannie,' admitted Iris, with tears in her eyes; 'and I am bemoaning it at the present moment, though I trust it will not be for long.'

'Gude forefend, mem!' Jeannie said so solemnly that Iris felt she must beat about the bush no longer.

'What do you think we were so tired of ourselves and of everything else, and so silly as to do, yesterday, in the gloaming ?'

'I think I ken, mem, said Jeannie, with a slightly reproachful accent. It appeared to her that Iris was not approaching the subject in a proper spirit ; it seemed as if the young lady were seeking to make out that there had been no set purpose and important reason why her party, which had dispersed so rapidly, had come together to the Borders. She was trying, from what motive it would be hard to say, to throw dust in Jeannie's wide-awake eyes, and pass off an incredible version of the story on a lass who had heard all about the grand old runaway marriages from her grandmother and her father and mother, who had herself seen humble, dis-creditable editions of the originals. More

than that, Jeannie had been told something
of what was going to take place by the other
franker young lady. Then the servant-girl
had rushed off and informed her master and
mistress, as in duty bound. Afterwards she
had gone back with them and others and
stood at the door of the room, and had heard
and seen the couple take each other for man
and wife, and join hands before witnesses in
due form, till the old lady, who did not look
offended either, put an end to the spectacle.

Jeannie was 'ill-pleased' by what struck
her as levity on the part of Iris, by her
trifling with the truth, to which she, Jeannie,
could swear, if need were. She commenced
re-wringing the drops of water from the next
towel with all the strength she possessed.
As she did so she said something plainly, to
show she would not be taken in ; for why
need the bride come to Jeannie and pretend
to confide in her, if the young lady was to
begin by speaking deceitfully ?

'The ither miss telled me as she passed me
on the stair that there was going to be a
marriage—I thocht she said she was going to
be married hersel', but I maun hae ta'en her
up wrang. An' I telled the maister, as I

behoved to do, and him and me and ithers in
the house stood at the door and saw the
waddin'. I may hae ta'en a liberty, mem,
but I did ye nae wrang, for there was naebody
pursuing to track you, and the mair witnesses
the better for you and yours. It is only when
the couple is like to be caught in the act,
or when there's mischief in the wind, that sic
a business is done hidlins.'

'But, Jeannie, there was no marriage,' insisted Iris. 'We were all in jest; we were
only making a little play out of your marriages.'

'Dinna tell me that grown-up men and
women, educate leddies and gentlemen,
would play sic a fule trick here!' cried
Jeannie incredulously, and well-nigh disdainfully.

She took up a pillow-case, and, holding it
up high, shook it as if in protestation, till she
brought down a shower of glistening drops
upon her brown hair and ruddy face. Then
she dropped her bare brown arms by her side
and said severely:

'It's nae matter o' mine if ony titled leddy
likes to lee—I beg your pardon, mem, I
micht hae fund a safter word, but I'm no

used to cringing ony mair than to dooble
tongues. My folk's a' honest and steady,
though they're only puir working men and
women, no sae muckle as a runawa' marriage
after a feein' market amang the whole lot o'
us, as the minister kens.   I put it to you,
mem—my leddy, I should say,' Jeannie corrected herself with malicious punctiliousness,
'though it may not be your wull to tak' your
title for a time—how can I or onybody in his
or her senses credit that you were a' daffin'
wi' ane anither at a wild game ?   It was
hardly fit for bairns, though it could be said
for them, for ae thing, they wouldna ken its
danger.   But, if you were just wilin' awa' the
close o' a rainy day, what for did the lave o'
the players melt awa' at aince like a snaw-ba',
and gang their wa's here and there, and leave
you and anither to bear the wyte ?   Weel-a-
wat it would hae been but richt and kind if
he had bidden still to bear his new-made wife
company ; however, there's an odds in the
manners o' gentle and simple, and he may hae
gone on a richt gude errand, and be back
again like a shot,' continued Jeannie, recovering her good-humour as she built up her
edifice to her satisfaction.

'You are wrong, Jeannie, altogether wrong,' was all Iris could say.

'Maybe sae,' answered Jeannie cautiously, not liking contradiction, but certainly doubtful where this ill-fitting, loose stone could come into the building. 'There was them that telled me when he came down in the mornin' and fund the feck of his friends gane, and saw the letter for you—the ane wi' the proper address—he grew as red as fire, and there was a glint in his een like a man who has gotten his heart's desire—be it a croon, or a lass, or a lad bairn. Neist he grew as white as death, and there were draps o' swate on his brow, as he gripped the table after the fashion o' a man who is riven in twa in his contention wi' his deadliest enemy. Syne he strachtened hissel' and gae a sech, and said he was ganging immediately. He wrat a letter or twa, and sent aff a messenger express wi' ane and laid the ither down, and cried for the time-table, paid the lawin' and walked oot without looking ower his shouther for his breakfast. But when he was as far as the yett what did he do afore he gaed?' asked Jeannie, resuming her tone of superior knowledge and settled conviction. 'He cam'

back and pat up siller—you'll no hinder the
maister frae kennin' what he was taking care
o'—and left it, like a canny young gudeman,
for the use o' his young gudewife, though he
did not ca' her sae, in case he should be detained longer than they foresaw, till he cam'
back to fetch her.   What mak' you o' that,
mem ?   Is that part o' a fule play ?   My
leddy, it is neither fair nor wise to seek to
darken the truth, the deil—that I should
name him—only kens wherefore, even to a
stranger lass, your inferior in warldly station, who yet would never harm you, but
would stand up for you if she got the chance,
and you needed her countenance.'

'Woman !' said Iris, in the vehemence of
her remonstrance and the extremity of the
moment, 'I would not depart from the truth
to save my life, any more than you would ;
and if you are a happy girl in being able
to boast of the virtue of your kindred, it
should not make you hard to others less
fortunate.   If you, a girl like myself, will
not believe me, where can I hope to find
trust?'

Overcome by the successive shocks of the
morning, Iris could only restrain by a great

effort the sob that rose to her throat and the tears to her eyes.

Jeannie's sharp eyes took in the signs, and the really kind heart of the girl, under her sturdy independence and shrewd observation, was touched.

'Na, dinna greet, my leddy, or mem, as you please; I'll believe onything reasonable you like to tell me. And gif there has been ony fause or base trick played upon you, I'll do my best to see you richted, though I'm but a servant lass; and sae will the maister and the mistress, which is mair to the purpose. I'm free to own they werena averse to me speerin' the ins and outs o' the story, if you gied me the chance. But if a living soul is to do you ony gude, mem, you maun speak oot, and keep naething back that has to do wi' the case.'

Iris could recognise the common-sense of the recommendation, and in the circumstances she felt she had better meet Jeannie's advances. After all, however much Iris's shrinking delicacy and the prejudices of her education recoiled from bestowing the confidence, there might well be worse confidants and counsellors than peasant-bred Jeannie,

with her perfect candour, honest maidenli-
ness, warm heart, and ready wit.

'It was as I said, Jeannie. Miss Dugdale,
my cousin, proposed to act one of your runaway marriages, and went to dress as a
runaway bride. But I did not like the play,
and I liked it least of all for her, because she
and one of the gentlemen—the taller and
fairer of the two—are sweethearts, though
she had never let him know that she cared
for him ; indeed, she had been teasing and
vexing him all the morning.'

Jeannie was intensely interested and appreciative. 'Biting and scarting are Scotch
folk's wooin',' she said. 'The young leddy
maun hae a drap o' gude Scotch blude in her
veins. There's mony a Maggie has " cuist
her head and looked fu' heich " to begin wi'.
But you mauna stand and wear yoursel' oot,
when you may hae eneuch afore you.' And
Jeannie nimbly emptied out her basket,
turned it over, and made Iris sit down upon
it. It did not signify that Jeannie was
in danger of losing the best of the morning
for bleaching and 'withering' her 'claes.'
In such a cause—the last grand marriage
that was ever likely to be enacted in the inn,

about which there might be trouble in time to come—even the mistress must allow, justified the wasted sunshine.

'It was not the man she liked in that way she had arranged should be the mock bride-groom.' Iris struggled gallantly to tell the story.

'Na, I could guess that,' commented Jeannie from her own experience and maidenly instinct.

'Mr. Acton—her real lover, I mean—was much hurt, and as he had to go off last night to see his family and join his ship—he is a sailor—there would have been no time for a reconciliation, and I fancied the thoughtless offence might have parted the two for ever.'

'For certain,' chimed in Jeannie deci-sively. 'If the chield had ony spunk. Eh! but she maun hae been a wilfu' madam—a heedless lassie.'

'I said I would be the bride instead of Miss Dugdale.'

'It was very gude o' you, mem, very gude, but unco fulehardy,' declared Jeannie, with her characteristic plain speaking. 'Them that devised the mischief ocht to hae run the risk and borne the brunt.'

'We had not the slightest idea, and I
cannot see it yet, that there was the least
danger, or that there could be a mistake
when none of us, neither bride nor bridegroom, nor the gentleman who consented
to say the words which you use in your
marriage ceremony, meant anything by it.'

'Then what for did they a' slip awa' like a'
knotless thread and leave you and the titled
gentleman, who maun hae been the bridegroom—'deed I seed him in the character wi'
my ain een, and a braw bonnie bridegroom
he looked—to suffer the scaith and the
scorn?' questioned Jeannie, with natural un-
masked impatience.

'It was the old lady, Lady Fermor, who is
grandmother both to me and Miss Dugdale,
that did it, and this is the painful part of the
story,' confessed Iris, with furious blushes.
'She has a great friendship for—for Sir
William Thwaite—you know his name
already. She wished greatly that there
should be a marriage between—between
him and either of her grand-daughters—first
one and then the other, but she had not been
able to bring it about. I suppose, but I
cannot tell, that she suddenly thought when

the temptation met her, for I cannot believe she brought us all this distance to lead us into a snare,' cried Iris, wringing her hands, ' she would make the jest look like earnest, deceive Sir William and frighten Miss Dugdale and me into imagining there was nothing left for us but to be married truly.'

'Oh, the auld bizzum! forgive me, mem, since she is your granny; but it is a sair pity when the auld, who suld be thinking o' a better place, hae neither conscience nor mercy, and are fit to sacrifice their bairns and their bairns' bairns if it will but compass some warldly plan of their ain. But what for did the other young leddy forsake you when you had done her sic a service?'

'I cannot tell, Jeannie,' said Iris sadly. ' But I think Lady Fermor and her maid must have misled my cousin up to the last moment, and then forced her away. If so, she will never rest till she finds me out; I can trust her for that.'

'You'll no think me impident, mem,' said Jeannie gravely, 'gin I say I canna a'thegither comprehend, though I dinna misdoobt your word. But I maun hae a' the airts and pairts o' the story to gie to them that may

help you.   There were letters left for you—
one o' them directed to Leddy Thwaite. You
opened baith, as gin you were free to do't—
more by token, the gentleman sent you money
for your use.'

It was unmistakable that Jeannie, though
genuinely indignant on Iris's account because
of what the young lady had told the girl, still
clung with a certain faith to the marriage,
partly because of the perplexing contradic-
tions she had alluded to, partly from a
natural reluctance to find that her first, and
it might be her last, example of a real grand
runaway marriage was likely to end in
smoke.

Iris stood aghast at these fresh compli-
cations.   Were the meshes of the net closing
round her ?   But she would strive to the
last to break through them.

' The letter addressed to Lady Thwaite was
in my grandmother's handwriting.   I knew
the handwriting and looked no farther.   I
never doubted it was written to me.'

' It was a thoosand pities you tore open
the envelope, for a written word gangs far in
law.   It makes nae odds what you did wi't
though you hae burnt it to ase, for a dizzen

folk could swear to the direction, and you
dauredna deny, you opened and read the
letter.'

' But it was not Sir William who addressed
it,' argued Iris, with a faint blush. ' I could
understand the name would be of moment
then. Think, Jeannie—anybody might write
a letter to you calling you by a name which
the writer had no right to give you, and you
might open the letter by mistake ; but the
unwarrantable name would signify nothing,
could not implicate you.'

' You forget, mem, the ither proofs,' said
Jeannie, who had the logical head and the
good parish schooling of many of her nation.

' I have a letter from Sir William Thwaite,
mentioning the marriage as a frolic, and
addressed to me as Miss Compton. Will that
letter not contradict the other ?'

' Weel, it suld do something,' granted
cautious Jeannie. ' But what aboot the
money for your use, mem ?'

' He sent it to me as a loan lest Lady
Fermor should have gone away and left
me without caring to ascertain whether I had
enough in my purse to pay my railway fare
in following her, or in going back to my

other friends in England. The precaution was justifiable,' said Iris, flashing out in the middle of her patient humility and holding up her fine little head in the old style. 'We had many expenses when we were in town. I had lent Miss Dugdale part of my last quarter's allowance, and I had not got the money for the next quarter—I was nearly penniless.'

'The heartless, hard-fisted auld sorry!' cried Jeannie, unable to restrain herself or even to offer an apology for her freedom of speech. 'Even a servant lass like me, gin she be wise, has maistly a pund or twa in the savings bank, or a couple o' croons in her kist to fa' back upon. But you puir young leddies, who mustna mint at working for your ain hands, are often as helpless as bairns, and mair hardly dealt wi' by evil paurents. Weel, mem, I hae you noo. I can follow your tale, though as sure's death it's gey daft-like; still it's within the boonds o' possibility, and it's no ay the daftest lass that gets into trouble. For my pairt I believe you ilka word, and sae micht jurymen and judge, if it were iver to get into a coort, though the auld leddy and her maid were to take

fause aiths—as you may swear the t' ain
wouldna stick at, and though the direction o'
the letter and the money and a' were brocht
in.   But losh ! mem, it was playin' wi' fire to
play at a Border marriage, on the very spot,
as gin the spirit o' the place possessed you.
The mere word o't micht stick to you and
bleck you to your deein' day.   What modest
lass, be she o' the laighest degree, would
care to gang into a coort and be speered and
back-speered by sniggering cunning black-
guards o' lawyers, aboot sic a job ?   Though
she were assured she would win her case,
altogether scaithless she could never again be.
As I said, the bare word o' the scandal would
stick to her.'

'But the story's far too absurd for a court
—who would carry it there ? not even **Lady
Fermor**,' pled Iris.

'You dinna ken,' said Jeannie, who preferred to look at all sides of a question, and
rather inclined to take the dark side ; 'one
can never tell how bools will row or what
ferlies may come to pass.   It micht be a score
or fifty years hence, when maist who could
hae telled the truth were gane, gin you had
married and had bairns, and ony money were

54—2

to be left to them, or to yoursel', and there
were ither claimants for the siller who heard
a souch lingering here o' what happened last
nicht, heth! it might cost your lads and
lasses their birthricht and cast shame on
their mither in her grave.'

'Oh, Jeannie, don't be a prophet of evil,'
implored Iris; 'and surely there is no need
to look so far forward.'

''Deed, that is just what there is need o',
and a far outlook is a grand thing. Could
you no mak' it up among yoursel's?' suggested
Jeannie, feeling her own responsibility, and
striving to give the most discreet advice to
the young English lady who had been so
simple in her uprightness, and was so gentle
in her tribulation. 'The titled gentleman
seems to be a manfu' mindfu' chap, and a
kind lad, taking it into account that he was
made a cat's-paw o' as weel as you, by the auld
leddy; for I fancy he wasna seeking the
price o' either o' you twa young leddies. I
say naething o' his being a grand match,
though when a' else is richt, siller, and a
lairdship, and a Sir before his name, are
God's gifts, and no to be lichtly despised by
ony prudent young leddy. He's faur frae ill-

faured, and you're a rale bonnie, civil-spoken young leddy, gin you'll let me say sae. You would mak' a braw young couple—your granny wasna far wrang there. Noo you're baith in the scrape, could you no think ower't and gin there be nae ither lad or lass standin' between, which makes a fell odds, could you twa no draw thegither and mak' the best o' what has happened? Whiles a prudent marriage is no the warst, and they say—

' "Happy's the 'ooin'
That's no long o' doin'." '

'Jeannie!' cried Iris, starting up as if the girl had been suborned by Lady Fermor to betray her grand-daughter's confidence which she had forced herself to give; 'how can you say such a thing, after I had proposed to be my cousin's substitute, as if I were offering myself to Sir William and throwing myself at the head of the man I rejected with scorn years ago?' presisted Iris, betrayed into casting down the last barrier of reserve she had jealously guarded.

'Keep me!' retorted Jeannie, 'here's another cat louped out o' the poke; no that it mak's ony great differ that I can see,

except to prove the heart's gudeness o' the
fine lad. Canny, mem! you're under nae
obligation to mind what I say, and troth I
dinna ken that I would do what I bade you
mysel'. But I maun mak' you aware of
something mair bearing on this wark. I
spoke to you about my auld granny who has
a' her wits aboot her, and minds fine yet o'
the grand runawa' marriages lang syne. She
bides wi' a single woman, a niece, a' her ain
bairns being dead lang syne, in a hoosie by
the road-side—the road that leads to the
station. Granny's an ill sleeper, and in summer
she often gets up by screich o' day, and puts
on her duds—she's fit for that yet—and
creeps to the door for a breath o' the caller
mornin' air. She was at the door this morning when the chaise with your leddy granny
passed, driving to the station, and my granny
has sent for me sin' syne. She thinks she
kenned the auld leddy. Granny had time to
look at her, for the horse next the hoosie had
gotten a stane in ane o' its fore-feet, and the
driver drew up and lichted down to pick it
oot, jist forenent granny. And the auld
leddy stood up and lent oot and banned him.
Granny will hae it she kenned baith the face—

though it was a hantle aulder—and the vice, as weel as the rampaging way. Granny says it was a leddy wha run away frae her man, and came wi' a lord as ill as hersel' to be buckled thegither on the Borders. But the man wha married the couples then resisted. He said it was clean against the law o' Scotland. Had the twa been bachelor and maid, or widower and widow, he could have jined them sae as nae man could lowse them; but he couldna an' he wouldna, and it would be as muckle as his place was worth, for him to marry siccan a couple. For the auld marriage law o' Scotland was to aid the helpless and defend the waik, but never to paunder to sin.'

CHAPTER XXXVIII.

A FLAG OF TRUCE.

Iris hung her head, and gave a piteous sigh at the lamentable coincidence; but before she could say a word she heard a voice she ought to know, and looking round she saw Marianne Dugdale hurrying down the 'loaning' to the bleaching-green. In a moment the swollen burn, the spread-out clothes, and the peasant figure of Jeannie, with her sleeves rolled up to her shoulders, and her linen apron, seemed to whirl round with Iris and vanish out of her sight; and the folly of last evening, and the abandonment and fright of this morning, to dwindle into the faintest confused dream.

'I have come back for you, Iris, as soon as I could,' Marianne kept saying; 'we must start immediately and join granny.'

'But I thought she had gone by the first train,' said Iris, in bewilderment.

'No; she missed it, by the greatest good luck. Oh! I've been so vexed; but we can't stay to talk about it now. We'll have plenty of time afterwards. It was a horrid shame; but she has heard from Sir William, and she has been forced to give in, stubborn as she is. Come along, like a duck. I've ordered out your trunk, which was left behind, too. I tell you Lady Fermor is half dead already, lying on a sofa in the waiting-room. We can't keep her there all day, and propose to travel by night. It would be the death of a woman at her age, and I'm sure we don't wish to have her death at our doors, whatever she may have done to us. The stableman is giving us fresh horses, and if we don't lose a moment we shall still be in time for the mid-day train.'

'The mid-day train!' cried Iris excitedly; 'but Sir William Thwaite is going by the mid-day train!'

'What although he is?' protested Marianne impatiently. 'He won't take a bite of us. We've travelled long enough with him to know he's perfectly inoffensive. Besides,

he's not at our station.   I told you he wrote
to granny ; and though she did not show me
the note, I believe he must have driven to
the next station.   Oh ! don't be a goose, Iris.
Let us get away instantly.'

There was little power of resistance left
in Iris, even if she had not seen, so far as she
was able to see, that Marianne's presence was
protection ; and that to rejoin Lady Fermor
at once, however disagreeable it might be for
both, would probably serve as the best refu-
tation to any attempt to maintain an outrageous story.   But Iris did not go without
bidding good-bye to Jeannie, thanking her
for her sympathy, and pressing on her a little
gift by way of remembrance.

'You see my friends have come back for
me, Jeannie.   It was all as I said.'

'Aweel, miss, I hope it may end as you
wuss,' said Jeannie doubtfully, as if she were
taking one of her grand far outlooks, and
seeing rocks and shoals ahead.   'I'm sure I
trust so for your sake,' much more cordially,
in answer to the wistful look in Iris's eyes.
'I think the maister wanted a word wi' you,
but he's awfu' thrang wi' a pairty o' strangers
seeking rooms for the fishing, and canna be

spoken to the noo, while the young leddy winna wait a blink. Since yer ain folk hae turned up again and are takin' you awa' wi' them, maybe it doesna matter. I'll keep your braw broochie and wear it, to mind me o' the young leddy who didna think hersel' aboon makin' a frien' o' me. Gude gang wi' you, mem ; an'—

> ' " May you live happy and dee happy,
>   And never drink out o' a dry cappie." '

Jeannie inadvertently wound up her farewell with one of the commonest couplets in use among her class for the benefit of a bride and bridegroom. It bore a startling resemblance to what it really was—a verse from a people's epithalamium.

Marianne would hardly wait for the leave-taking. She dragged Iris away to the chaise, and Iris did not look back—she felt there was no need. The steep-roofed white house with the red roses and the honeysuckle about its windows, standing in the paddock among the old trees, which she had greeted at first sight with so light a heart, seemed as if it were branded on her memory. She might long to efface the scene and forget its very existence, but it would stand out clearly

before her so long as memory itself was left
to her.

When the girls were in the chaise, the door
shut, and the horses started ; neither the
rapid motion nor any amount of jolts on the
country road could keep Marianne's mouth
shut or take away her breath.

'What a dreadful affair it has been ! How
much better granny has acted the wicked
grandmother than we performed the marriage
ceremony !   Could you have believed it
possible for so old a woman to be possessed
by such an evil spirit ?   I don't mean evil in
a general way, to which one has got accustomed—I mean daring, defiant wrong-doing !
But I must tell you about my share in it.
Of course, when I was awakened in the
middle of the night, and told we were going
to the station, to breakfast at the railway inn
and start with the early train—after I had
got over the impression that King Lud had
come back, and the alarm that the house
had gone on fire, and the fear that granny
was taking leave of her senses—I was so cold,
and sleepy, and stupid, that I might have
been standing on my head all the time.
Soames ran up every five minutes to beg me

to make haste; and as I was getting so much attention I thought you were in good time and were with Lady Fermor. I never missed you till we were in the chaise, and even then I imagined that it was by a blunder you were being left behind, just as I concluded Sir William was on the box. I cried out to granny that you were not there, and I called you by name, but she had the strength to pull me down on the seat, and put her hand on my mouth. I was so taken by surprise that I could not free myself. Besides, all the time she was chuckling and laughing so as to put me off my guard, and persuade me the whole manœuvre was some good joke, of which I should presently see the point, and then I might laugh with my neighbours. But when the explanation came it was a string of cock-and-bull nonsense, of which I did not believe one word. She said Sir William Thwaite and you had been lovers years ago. What a story, Iris! when you were never more than friends—the most matter-of-fact, good friends. She told me that you had not behaved well to him— another story!—but had trifled with him, and pretended to put him off. Then he went away in a pet and made a low marriage. But all that was over, and now you wanted to make it up with him; and you would have done so a great deal sooner if I had not stood in the way—she had the coolness to say so. She assured me that your coming in as the bride last evening was not to serve me, or anybody save yourself, though I had been so silly as to be taken in. You intended the step as a piece of encouragement to Sir William to come on again. I might be sure he understood it perfectly and accepted it, so now you both understood each other; and it would be the kindest service your friends could render you—it would be doing by one's neighbour as one would be done by one's self, to go away and leave you to each other. You were really married in the Scotch fashion, and if you cared to be married over again in church with flying colours, you could be so any day, though it was not at all necessary. Everybody knew that Border marriages were perfectly good in the eyes of the law. Now, Iris, did you ever here such a rigmarole? Would you not have thought that granny, however full of malice, had too much brains to concoct such sensational trash?'

Iris sat dumb for a moment, then she asked desperately :

' And what did you say, and do ?'

'Oh! I did not say " Gammon !" and " Tell that to the marines !" as our boys would have said. I was so disgusted and enraged on my own account that I behaved beautifully ; yes, I did, Iris. I was perfectly quiet and polite. I said it was an entire mistake—I knew it to be so ; and that the moment I got to the station I would look out for a curricle and go back and fetch you. I would explain everything to the station-master, and if he refused to attend to me I would demand to be taken before a magistrate and tell my story. She and Soames might go on if they pleased ; you and I would follow after. We were old enough to take care of ourselves ; indeed, I was not sure that we should not manage it better than some of our elders could do it for us. Anyway, I would be torn to pieces by wild horses before I entered the train without you. She gave an ugly grin, and asked if I wanted Sir William for myself. But I was her match for once. I said she-was at liberty to think so if she chose. She neither called me a

chit nor a baggage, nor proposed to put me
out and leave me in the middle of the road,
which would have been awkward, as you can
see for yourself, my dear. There are such
ruts and pools of water, that even if I had
taken no wrong turning—and Sir William
always says I am without the bump of locality
—I should have wasted ever so much time
trudging back for you. I had made up my
mind she meant to give me up as a raging
lunatic before I could open my mouth to the
stationmaster ; but the train steamed out of
the station just as we drove up. Then she
was so stiff, and had such difficulty in getting
out of the chaise, that I could not leave her
to Soames, who looked frightened out of her
wits. I had to help, and see poor, miserable
old granny laid on a sofa, and order brandy
and tea for her. She was nearly two hours
in coming round. I think now it was a trick,
but at the time I got as frightened as Soames,
and dared not turn my back. What brought
her to herself at last was a man on horseback,
with a letter from Sir William Thwaite to
her. Then, sure enough, she looked like
herself in a second, sat up, and read the
letter. I think she said something about a

weak fool, who did not know his own mind, and could not play his game, though the cards were put into his hands. At last she turned round and told me, " Girl, do as you will ; you are a deluded idiot for your pains. Do you think Sir William has been making up to *you* all these weeks ? He may have given you reason to think so, to serve his own purpose ; but he has been sighing and dying for that saint and fool of a cousin of yours since first he set eyes on her. There is no accounting for tastes. But if he is not man enough to grasp his prey when it is within his reach he is not worth my help. Take your own way, and much good may it do you. But remember, if you are not back before the next train, I shall start with Soames, and my dutiful grandchildren may find their way back to me as they can." As if we could not, Iris ! Never mind her, darling ; don't look so horribly cast down. Why should we care ? Don't we know granny by this time ? And though she is a great misfortune to everybody connected with her—nobody can deny that—still, don't you think it is worst of all for herself ? And you have me ; I have not failed you.'

'I cannot help caring, Marianne,' said Iris, with a wan wavering smile. 'It was so cruel.'

'But it is not as if there had been anything in it, as if Sir William had cared for you, or you for him, that you should take it so to heart, and not laugh at it now that it is over, as at any other passing annoyance. Iris, was there ever anything in it—any foundation for what she said? Have you been hiding the truth from me all this time?' cried Marianne, dropping the rare caressing touches she had been indulging in, drawing back into her corner of the chaise, and staring at her cousin suspiciously and jealously.

'There was nothing to conceal,' said Iris faintly, 'except that long ago, as it seems to me now, when Sir William first came to Whitehills, we were thrown a good deal together. Grandmamma encouraged it, and wished to make a match between us, until he fancied he cared for me, and asked me to marry him, and I refused him—that is all, Marianne.'

'And enough too,' said Marianne sarcastically; 'and I suppose you also refused Ludovic Acton?'

'Oh no!' declared Iris, with a weary little laugh, 'for the very good reason that I never had the opportunity. King Lud, to my knowledge, never cared for any girl save one.'

'I don't know,' said Marianne discontentedly; 'I feel as if I had lost my faith in mankind, and womankind to boot. Why, I might have fallen in love with Sir William!' she exclaimed naïvely.

'When he would doubtless have returned the compliment.'

'No, not if he had begun by sighing and dying for you, as granny said. I am not an utter fool, Iris,' protested Marianne hotly, 'though I may be a simpleton in believing in those I thought my friends. You are not a girl likely to be forgotten by a man like Sir William Thwaite. I should never have dreamed of putting you out, any more than of your keeping all this back from me, when I believed I knew everything about you, even when I told you—what I told last evening.'

'My dear little cousin, be reasonable,' Iris exerted herself to entreat. 'The story was an old one, dead and buried for years.

Was it for me to dig it up out of its grave, to go and boast that an unlucky man had once put himself into my power, and I had abused his confidence after many days? Would you have had me do that? You could see for yourself that there was nothing between Sir William Thwaite and me, that we were no more than friends.'

Marianne was silent for a long time, with her dark eyes cast down and a lowering brow. She suddenly looked up, and it darted into her head that Iris's little face had grown colourless in the course of twelve hours, that there were dark rings under her eyes, and that her hands trembled as they lay loosely in her lap. She had been insulted and persecuted almost more than she could bear, and here was the girl in whose favour Iris had interposed, for whose happiness she had been so concerned, even to exposing herself to misconception, in order to secure Marianne's welfare, proceeding to persecute the victim, in turn, out of sheer unworthy vanity and exacting pride.

'I am a heartless creature, worse than I could have thought possible,' Marianne cried. 'I beg your pardon, my pet, if you will let

me call you so—you who were so good to me ;
and it must have cost you much more than I
guessed.'

'Yes, it cost me something,' said Iris
simply, 'because I did not like the play in
itself, and it was inevitable that there should
be some awkwardness. But neither of us
knew what we were doing, or had any notion
what it might lead to. Don't speak of it,'
said Iris, with a shiver ; 'I cannot talk of it
yet.'

'Just let me say one thing : if I had been
in your place, and she had done it to me—I
suppose she would all the same ; I think she
wanted Sir William to have me if he could
not have you—and if I had quarrelled with
King Lud, and he had come to hear the
garbled story—oh ! Iris, Iris, I should have
been lost. My dear, my dear, I ought to go
down on my knees to thank you, and I do
thank you with all my heart.'

'I know it, and it is some comfort to have
served you.'

'At your own expense ! Oh ! I must do
something for you—not that I can ever repay
you, but to prevent your being a scapegoat
for me. If not, I shall break my heart for

having brought you into such trouble, and he will never forgive me after all, for he is as fond of you as if you were one of his sisters.'

'Don't speak of it,' Iris repeated imploringly.

'It drives me wild when I think I have been deceived,' confessed Marianne ingenuously, after another pause ; 'not that you deceived me—at least, you could not help it. But I wonder if it was all a piece of imagination on my part—it is better to know the truth, though it will make me ashamed — that Sir William liked me a little ?'

'I am sure he liked you very much,' said Iris promptly ; 'you were so bright, you made him chaff you and laugh with you as I never saw him do with anyone else. You know he is rather silent and serious for a young man.'

'Yes,' said Marianne doubtfully ; 'but I thought he sometimes looked at me sadly, as well as kindly, as if he would like to take care of me—you know what I mean—I dare say he pitied me. He knew granny of old, and he thought I was not in very good

hands, and he might be a better protector ;
but that would have been a great mistake,'
shaking her head, 'and I believe he was
thinking of his old love, his true love, yesterday when I brought you to him. A great
glow came into his face—I was looking more
at King Lud, naturally, but I saw it ; and
don't you remember he said " I will," as if his
heart was in his mouth ? I felt it at the
time with a sense of something odd, though
it went out of my head the next moment.
Could he have fancied for an instant that the
scene was real ? Then what a temptation to
him granny's behaviour must have been !
Dearest Iris, can the jest not become earnest,
and you two friends be as happy as King Lud
and I shall be some day ?' cried Marianne,
clasping her hands on her knees and leaning
over to her cousin.

'For shame's sake, don't talk such nonsense, Marianne !' said Iris, with asperity at
last. 'You know I offered myself to him,
though it was in compliance with your foolish
arrangement—not mine. You ought to be
aware that there is no foundation for your
suggestion ;' and Marianne was silenced for
once.

The girls arrived in time for the train, and Lady Fermor had so far recovered that she was on the platform. She looked them over, then spoke to Iris with an effrontery which was almost without parallel.

'So you have taken us in, Iris,' she said lightly and airily, with a double meaning in her words, and yet as if nothing had happened.

It gave her grand-daughter strength to assert herself.

'You have not kept your promise to me, Lady Fermor,' Iris said. 'You might have told me that you wished to get rid of me, and I should have gone away honourably, as I did before. I shall go away again as soon as I can.'

'Without asking my leave, no doubt?' exclaimed her ladyship, raising her eyebrows.

'I did ask your leave, and now I may take it for granted.'

'As you will, Miss Compton. I am too old to parley with you.'

It was a silent party—down to Marianne Dugdale — that travelled across the grey Border moors, through the more fertile por-

tion of Dumfriesshire, up to the heathery hills
of Annandale.

When the train drew up in the Moffat
Station, long shadows were falling across the
platform; but Iris, who sat by the nearest
door, distinguished a well-known figure in
the shadow, and drew back aghast. Sir
William Thwaite had come on from Dumfries, and was standing like a sentinel on
duty—with only a heightened colour to indicate any trace of discomposure—prepared to
hand the party out.

'You here, Thwaite?' cried Lady Fermor,
in loud challenge. 'Well, we've been playing at cross-purposes, it seems; but it is
lucky that we have shaken ourselves right,
come together, and all turned up at our
destination. Have you made any inquiry
about the moor—whether the birds are shy
or not?'

He had no reply for her, beyond helping her
carefully out of the carriage and leading her
away. By that time Iris understood what his
change of plans meant. His presence there
as well as hers was best for making everything
be as it had been, and for putting out of mind
the *mauvais quart d'heure* which had inter-

vened.   If he had not come immediately, and
the two had not met again without delay, she
felt as if their re-encountering each other
would have been intolerable.   Now it was
still so much a matter of course, and the
true gloss was so impressed on an idle farce,
that before he parted from them in the lobby
of the hotel, Iris could go up to him in the
presence of Lady Fermor, Marianne, and
Soames, and gently return to him his little
packet, saying :

'Thank you very much, Sir William; you
see I have not needed your loan.'

CHAPTER XXXIX.

A SUITOR.

For the next few days the party returned to their former habits, Sir William not availing himself immediately of his right to constitute 'a gun' on a neighbouring moor.

The sole evidence that there had been any disturbance of the company's tranquillity remained in a certain constraint which clung about their intercourse, a disinclination to allude to their halt on the Borders, and an utter avoidance of a topic which had been much discussed before.

Yet the forbidden topic cropped up occasionally, even without Lady Fermor's instrumentality. When the ladies and their squire were strolling about the streets of the little town, and had come back to the street in which their comfortable old inn was situated, some conjecture was hazarded about its age.

Marianne Dugdale predicted they would not
find an old inn in Scotland of a later creation
than Prince Charlie's time. A respectable
tradesman passing by, and catching the tenor
of the conversation, took it upon him to
supply the date and oblige the party with a
gratuitous piece of information.

'Auld Lord Dundonald, the great sailor,
came on here with his bride after their runawa'
marriage. Ye may mind the marriage was
disputed in a court of law after Tam
Cochrane had bidden a long fareweel, baith
to his honours and his disgrace, and my
leddy was a bitter-tongued, weedow woman,
driven, puir sowl, to fecht baith for and
against her ain sons.'

'The folly is in the air,' said Lady Fermor
sarcastically; 'shall we consult your safety,
Thwaite, and flee back to England?'

'I do not know myself in any danger, my
lady,' said the person addressed, stiffly and
sternly, while Marianne talked fast to Iris
of climbing the hill behind the town, which
was somehow connected with hanging and
the gallows.

It was not the anticipation of the exercise
which deepened to a painful scarlet the rose

in the delicately tinted face, and then drained
the colour away before a sudden pallor. It
was the sense of unmerited humiliation and
affront, and a terrified recollection of Jeannie
the maid at the Border inn's warning with
regard to the slow, steady, poisonous scandal
that might distil, drop by drop, through
generations, and break out with fatal viru-
lence in the far future.

Still, whether to drown care and escape
unpleasant recollections, the younger members of the party were as indefatigable as
ever in their business of sight-seeing. They
walked, rode, and drove to the pretty mineral
well in its nook among the hills, to ' lone St.
Mary's Loch,' with its silver strand, where
the images of Scott and Hogg and Words-
worth for the moment effaced all private
phantoms, to the spot where Tweed, Clyde,
and Annan are near akin in their origin, to
the weird lichen-covered oaks of Lochwood,
like trees of another world, to the colossal
green hollow known as ' the Devil's Beef-
tub,' to ' fair Kirkconnel Lea,' the scene of
the most wildly tragic and deeply pathetic of
Scotch ballads, which greatly took the young
people's fancy. To them the Helen who in-

terposed between her lover and his murderous
rival and received the shot destined for another in her own tender bosom, was the
truest of heroines, so that English strangers
of another generation could echo from the
heart that unspeakably fond and piteous
lament :

> ' Oh ! would I were where Helen lies,
>   For night and day on me she cries ;
>   Oh ! would I were where Helen lies,
>   On fair Kirkconnel Lea.'

On the little company's return from one of
their excursions they were amazed to find the
big body, big face, and sandy moustache of
King Lud in the man who was standing
smoking and looking out for them at the inn
door.

He had done more than keep his word.
He had spoken of seeing them again before
he sailed ; but that was comparatively a
vague prospect ; he had said nothing of returning so soon to make up their party and
finish their excursion. He looked solemn in
answer to the gay banter which Marianne
Dugdale, after an instant of silent delight,
was able to rain upon him.

' Were all your friends from home, Mr.

Acton ? Has your ship sailed without you ? Did you think we should be robbed and murdered without the protection of your doughty arm in the old land of Border reivers ? I could do better than that if I tried—like the duchess in Wonderland, I could make myself picturesquely charming, and come-over the Scotch loons with my soft English tongue.'

Iris, whose nerves had been thoroughly shaken, was divided between two sources of apprehension. Had Ludovic Acton taken it into his head to institute inquiries, read up information, and somehow discovered for himself the dangerous nature of their late entertainment, and had he come all the way from the Rectory, during the small amount of leave that was likely to remain to him, to put her on her guard, to volunteer his evidence, and to save everybody from sorrow and injury ?

Sometimes Iris was driven to believe that if the step could be taken without further publicity, the greatest safety for all might lie in a deposition made before a magistrate, which even Lady Fermor ought to sign. The next moment Iris was tempted to think that she was making a mountain out of a

mole-hill, and grossly exaggerating a trifle
which would never be called in question. If
Ludovic did not mean to act as a mediator,
was his mother worse ? and, if so, why had he
quitted her ?

The first time the old friends were alone
for a few minutes, King Lud cleared up the
mystery, his manner presenting a nice blend-
ing of sheepishness and burning anxiety. He
had got his promotion ; he was now a captain
in her Majesty's navy, with his appointment
to a ship a matter of days. But before these
days were ended he must avail himself of his
promotion to bring to a close the suspense
which, he maintained, was worse than sharks,
icebergs, and torpedoes all taken together.

Of course he could not run away with
Marianne Dugdale, though they were in
Scotland. He was so bent on his narrative
that he did not notice how Iris winced at the
dry joke. Neither could the most sanguine
man in his profession have hoped to marry
her before sailing. Even a middy who was
not particular might have found a difficulty
in getting up his kit so instantaneously as
that otherwise delectable step implied.

Miss Dugdale could not do without her

trousseau. Besides, he loved her too well to hurry and harass her ; if ever woman deserved to be patiently and loyally waited for she deserved it. But if Miss Dugdale, and her friends for her, would condescend to have anything to say to him, would consent to an engagement, he did not think, unless she was less freshly simple and modest in her tastes, less nobly and gloriously unworldly, than he believed her to be, that the engagement need be very long.

He could show flattering letters from some of the swells of the Admiralty and good-natured commendations from his old commanders, which he had never so much as given to the family at home to read and exult over, because, naturally, his people would think a great deal too much of such bosh, and he hated bounce and palaver. It would be the first time that he had counted on them as any good, if they would satisfy Marianne Dugdale and her friends of what he thought he could venture to engage, that a fair, steady rise in his profession lay before him.

He had not let the grass grow beneath his feet. Modest, retiring King Lud, under the influence of the great passion of his young manhood, had already rushed down to Devonshire, introduced himself to Mr. Dugdale, and interviewed him. The spick-and-span captain had explained his not too elevated but hopeful position, and requested the father's permission to address his eldest daughter.

The poor gentleman was neither propitious nor unpropitious. He was engrossed with his own affairs, to which the marriage of one of his daughters belonged certainly, but only in a subsidiary degree. Engulfed in the bottomless swamp of agricultural difficulties, Mr. Dugdale saw no light upon his future beyond a will-of-the-wispish expectation from his brother in India, who, though he was a mighty personage in his sphere, had so many sons of his own, that he might well decline to adopt another family. Young Acton might end by becoming a rear-admiral, when Marianne would have done very well for herself. Even if he stopped short with being a commodore he was not to be despised. Nay, a naval captain's pittance did not mean such starvation to a small family as a country gentleman's reduced rents from an estate groaning under a burden of mortgages, threatened ruin to the head of the house with his helpless wife and daughters. The officer and his wife would begin housekeeping with only a couple of mouths to fill, while Mr. Dugdale had nearly half-a-dozen to satisfy.

On the other hand, what had the dowager Lady Fermor to say on the matter? By making a marriage displeasing to the late Lord Fermor's testatrix she might be lost —not only to Marianne, but to the whole family of Dugdale.

Mr. Dugdale had a natural affection for his daughter; but he could not afford the sacrifice. In the end the eager suitor was referred to his father's prodigal parishioner.

This sentence filled King Lud with chagrin —well-nigh hopelessness.

' I know she has other views for her granddaughter,' he groaned in Iris's ear ; ' and she is right so far, that Marianne Dugdale deserves the best match in the kingdom—or a throne, if it would make her happier. Do you think there is the slightest chance for me in applying to the old lady ?'

Iris could not in sincerity say she had an exalted opinion of his chance in that quarter ; but she managed to remark with some am-

biguity she did not think Lady Fermor had
any definite designs at present for the disposal
of Marianne.

'There is Thwaite,' alleged King Lud
gloomily, 'almost a member of the family.
He has been its cavalier ever since Lady
Fermor and Miss Dugdale came up to
town.'

Had King Lud forgotten that Sir William
had been the favourite cavalier at Lambford
long before Marianne Dugdale showed her
face there? Was the young fellow blinded
by his own feelings? Had his mind con-
tracted; had he, in fact, no mind to spare for
any interest before and after Marianne Dugdale's appearance on the scene? It was
clear that he had heard nothing of the sequel
to the Border play in which he had taken
part—nor was he likely to hear, Iris was
thankful to think, unless his relations to the
family became very intimate.

'There would be disgusting advantages
in that match,' King Lud bemoaned himself.

'But Marianne is not mercenary,' Iris re-
minded him.

'Of course not; her dear vagaries, her

sweet waywardness and irresistible originality are all utterly destitute of mercenari-
ness.'

Iris laughed and nodded ; it was comical
to her to hear King Lud, who had been wont
to take things easy, by his own confession
violently in love.

'But Thwaite himself is a good fellow, for
all that has come and gone. I always liked
him. If he made a great mistake, went
wrong and smarted for it, he has come
honourably through a lengthened probation
since then. She is just the generous girl to
long to make up to him for what he has
suffered, to glory in overlooking his small
deficiencies, and be willing to risk herself to
keep him straight. No,' said Ludovic Acton
in dolefully magnanimous self-depreciation,
'I cannot pretend to Thwaite's advantages
in any respect. Why, even in the matter of
looks, he has it all on his side. He is a comely,
well - drilled lout, while I'm a whey - faced,
moon-faced—you can't deny, Iris, she has
compared my face to the moon !—clumsy sea-
lubber.'

Iris laughed till the tears came into her
eyes ; she wanted so much to comfort and

encourage him without breaking faith, and without buoying him up with false hopes where Lady Fermor was concerned.

'I think I may say if grandmamma has not entirely given up contemplating White-hills as a possible establishment for Marianne, she has not been looking at it in that light very lately.'

'Oh, thank you, Iris ; you are a good soul. I don't wonder that Marianne adores you,' said Ludovic as gratefully as if Iris had gone far to secure to him the passionately coveted boon. 'Only Marianne might spare a little common civility to a fellow who adores her.

> ' " Although she is forced to dissemble her love,
>   Why need she kick him downstairs ?" '

'Have patience,' Iris told him. 'Do they know at the Rectory ? What does Lucy think ? What does the Rector say ? Is the mother pleased ?'

She feared that even in King Lud's case the new love might have so eclipsed the old as to cause him to fail those who had so long held the first claims on him. It was balm to her gentle, faithful heart to hear

him say, with such ready confidence that
it was clear he had not guessed her suspicion :

'Oh, my people are as good as gold, as
usual. They say, if my happiness is concerned, that is everything. They are only
longing to make her acquaintance. What a
fool I am to speak of her as if she were certainly mine ! They hardly saw anything of
her before she went to town with Lady
Fermor. I can depend upon them doing
everything they can to befriend her when I
am away.'

'Happy man ! at least you have acted
on the most manly, straightforward principles, and whatever comes of it, you will
have the comfort of that reflection,' said Iris
warmly.

But the newly-made captain did not see
what else he could have done, therefore it
looked as if, in the result of failure, he would
miss even the small consolation of an ap-
proving conscience. It was left for his old
friend Iris to take the assurance that King
Lud's behaviour had been worthy of himself,
and that in one way or another his reward
would not fail him.

The reward was more and more according to his heart than Iris or anyone else would have dared to hope. Strange to say, Lady Fermor did not oppose the engagement, beyond saying that she thought it as foolish as such contracts usually were. But if the young pair chose to enter into this one, she would not interfere. She craved leave to inform Captain Acton, in case of awkward mistakes, that her grand-daughter, Marianne Dugdale, would have no more money from her than a couple of hundred pounds to buy her trousseau, if she ever needed one, and perhaps another couple of hundreds to buy her mourning on the death of the speaker. She had never intended to give Marianne more, unless on a contingency of which there had ceased to be any possibility. She would write to Mr. Dugdale to this effect.

Such a communication, however disappointing to the unfortunate landowner, was a virtual withdrawal of all opposition to the engagement. The truth was, that Lady Fermor did not believe in engagements, short or long, and never had cared a straw for Marianne Dugdale, except as a living toy to amuse the old lady, and an instrument of vengeance upon Iris Compton.

King Lud was free to address his mistress, yet even the freedom might have had a disastrous issue but for recent events, and the knowledge that the suitor would sail and very likely be in another hemisphere within the month. If there were any elements of character in common between Lady Fermor and Marianne Dugdale, the old and the young woman were totally unlike in this, that what the former counted on—correctly as far as her own instincts went—as certain sources of the dissolution of the engagement, formed the best conditions not merely for its present attainment, but for its permanent safety, where Marianne Dugdale had to do with it.

A lover far away, in peril of water and of deadly foreign climates even in times of peace, in the monotony and deprivations of an officer's duties on board ship, on a long cruise with only her word to rely on, her love and constancy to defend his cause, was likely to prove a far more formidable, irresistible wooer to Marianne Dugdale, a far surer pre-tender to her hand after years of separation,

than he would have been had he figured as
a man endowed with many of the good things
of fortune, dangling at her elbow, pleading
his claims every day.

Marianne was taken unawares. She
laughed and pouted, and even cried a little,
as if she were a very ill-used little person ;
then suddenly threw down her arms and
surrendered at discretion, making no terms,
beyond the right of teasing King Lud, which
the infatuated fellow was only too content,
according to ancient example, to let her do.
Even this remnant of power was in danger of
being wrested from her grasp, every time his
approaching departure crossed her mind and
clouded over the whole universe to her.
When Marianne began to hate post-time,
and to shiver at the reading out of naval
intelligence, her season of maidenly haughti-
ness and defiance was well-nigh over. The
' Lady of the Lea' was practically vanquished.

It was something to see a good fellow and
an innocent child so radiantly happy as those
two, though his lapsing leave was to subdue
their happiness long before the summer had
ended ; to know mortals so blest, though

the curse which heralded the ejection from Eden was dogging their steps. The man and woman would soon quit the garden, but their love would help them in the struggle with the thorns and thistles of earth, and make it easier for them to find the strait gate and narrow way which lead to a nobler and more enduring Paradise. Lady Fermor called the pair a couple of lunatics ; but Iris caught herself and Sir William regarding the two with the mild, patient benignity of true guardians and sponsors.

There was no evidence of resentment on Sir William's part on account of his faintly and fitfully foreshadowed office of 'guide, philosopher, and friend' to Marianne Dugdale being filched from him. If a kind of wistful look came into his blue eyes at times, it did not interfere with the perfect cordiality of his congratulations to King Lud and the young lady, and she received such demonstrations better from him than from anyone else, Iris not excepted.

It seemed as if nothing were to be wanting to the happiness of the lovers. King Lud had been proudly and affectionately desirous that, if it could be managed, Marianne should

go on a visit to the Rectory before he got his
sailing orders.   Included in the desire was
the natural longing to take leave of her in
his father's house, and to consign her under
the ordeal to the tender keeping of those
who   would   be   sharing   her   sorrow   with
her.

Even this wish was granted.   Lady Fermor became complacent to an almost alarming extent ; Marianne might go since she had
got her father's permission.   The old lady
even volunteered to render the project more
feasible by sending Soames to chaperon the
lovers, and bring back some articles of dress
which Soames's mistress wished her maid to
get from Lady Fermor's wardrobe at Lambford.

So this idyl disappeared from the contem-
plation of the edified spectators at Moffat,
and anything more they were to learn of it,
in the meantime, must be from letters—
Marianne's hurried but highly appreciative
announcement of her safe arrival and good
reception ; Lucy Acton's kind, if more composed and modified reports.   Yes, Marianne
was a dear girl, and it was delightful to see
King Lud so exultant ; who could resist it ?

Her father and mother, not to say Lucy herself, might have preferred another choice on Ludovic's part; but without question the principals in the compact were entitled to follow their inclinations so long as these were perfectly lawful. Marriages were made in heaven, and she thought—nay, she was sure, Ludovic's would prove a happy marriage in all essentials.

Marianne was original and a little wilful. She had found a broken mouse-trap, which had exercised her spirit a good deal. She had sent the children to fetch all the mouse-traps in the house to be inspected by her, and had set about mending them on the spot, so that Gerald was her chum from that moment. She had insisted, and carried her point, that she could repair the hinge of the gate without the aid of the smith. She had taken the Rector quite by surprise when he found her engaged on the job.

He had always been so fond of womanly softness and domesticity—apart from parish work—and so horrified by women's clamouring for equality with men, just because he would, of his own free will, defer to every woman worthy of the name, and pay her homage, which was surely a great deal better than treating her as his equal. However, Marianne had assured him that though she liked to be her own smith and carpenter, she did not think she had a vocation for stump oratory. She would never propose to do anything save sit in the Rectory pew and let him fill his own pulpit.

After that explanation, Marianne had got round the Rector by looking out his sermons for him, and practising the hymns he liked best in order to help the choir in church. She had objected to advanced arithmetic being so little taught in the school, and had proposed to introduce mathematics; and though Lucy was convinced Marianne was wrong in the last proposal, she daresayed the reformer might be right in the first. Lucy had come to think so since Marianne had been of the greatest use to Mrs. Acton in making up her subscription books—Marianne had done it so cleverly, and rendered every sum so beautifully clear and without a mistake in five minutes.

She had won all the hearts of her children —of the boys especially—at the school-feast. As for the curates, she saved her, Lucy, an immense amount of trouble ; for Marianne could twist them round her finger, and did so without once provoking King Lud to jealousy.

Yes, they all liked dear Ludovic's future wife very much, and Lucy was convinced that, though there might be a little hitch here and there—as where was there not in human relations ?—still the family circle into which the stranger had entered, instead of being divided into hostile factions with the members set against each other by her means, would continue as united and attached as ever.

It was plain the Actons were behaving well, as might have been expected from them. They were making the best of their son and brother's engagement to Marianne Dugdale, and so taking the wisest course to preserve his and their dignity and happiness.

Iris could not help smiling a little at the Rector's little discomfiture. She thought of what his similes must have been—of the lily which his sailor boy had been permitted to gather and wear in his breast ; of the dove which was not frightened to nestle in his

blue jacket, and would fly in spirit with him
over many a league of sea, to abide with him
in calm and tempest, till he should return to
redeem his pledge.   Then Iris pictured how
the worthy man must have been taken aback
when he came upon Marianne in her blouse
and the nearest approach to a leather apron
she could improvise, hammering away like
another Jael, with her chubby hands soiled
—as Jael's need not have been—and perhaps
a smut on Marianne's face ; or when he must
entertain a rueful suspicion that the east
wind had got into his future daughter-in-law's
temper, and that both she and her neighbours must suffer a fair share of discomfort
till the *mal d'humeur* was by some means
routed.

But Iris could also rejoice that her old
friends were vindicating what she had long
known of their virtues. She could be un-
grudgingly glad that Marianne was to have
everything in her favour, every chance of
developing into a good woman : an early
engagement to a fine fellow in the best sense
of the words, the hearty support of all his
friends as well as of her own, an absence
which in its nature could only make the warm

heart grow fonder, and in all probability a happy marriage the next time King Lud came home.

How strange it is, when all is said, that without reference to merit, so much of earthly sunshine, peace, and smooth sailing is granted to some, while to others is given an equal amount of the shadow of death, trouble, and a stormy passage through life! Yet could Iris take upon her to say, that the first who received all the smiles and none of the frowns of fortune—so called—were really the favoured and honoured voyagers, instead of those who grew strong by many a tussle with winds and waves, and came in at last, battered, but with their colours flying, to the haven where they would be?

CHAPTER XL.

DATING as nearly as possible contemporaneously with the departure of Ludovic Acton and his promised wife under the staid wing of Soames, there began for Iris one of the strangest experiences of her tried life. She was alone with Lady Fermor and Sir William Thwaite. Lady Fermor continued in the blandest mood. Whether she were seeking to atone for her late outrage, whether she were 'fey,' according to the old Norse superstition, and her last days had come, there could be no question of her indulgence to her grand-daughter and her kindness to Sir William, even when they crossed her will and thwarted her plans.

But along with the old lady's bluff good-humour there commenced to peep out an inference drawn by Lady Fermor which was

almost intangible in its expression at first.
But the suggestion grew always more overpowering and all-pervading, while it could
not be boldly repelled, because it was never
distinctly stated. It was a subtle, entangling,
bewildering implication, leading to a spirit of
perturbation and confusion on the part of
those who could not deny what was not
charged against them. They feared so much
as to admit the hint, lest the faintest whisper of its existence should lend tangibility
to the light material and afford a basis for a
whole towering edifice of doubt and suspicion.

Lady Fermor had boasted that no one
should be able to say she had not taken care
of her grand-daughter's morals and manners.
Having been an unscrupulous evil-doer in
her own day, she was all the more alive to
avoiding the very appearance of evil in her
descendant. Her grandmother had therefore
insisted on strict decorum for Iris Compton
from her childhood. Suddenly the old lady
relaxed her rule. She treated the two young
people, who were still with her, as if they
were a couple of children, or the nearest
relations. She would have sent them out, in

the intervals of Sir William's sport, on the
longest *tête-à-tête* rambles and riding excursions without so much as a groom to bear
them company. When, because of the un-
accustomed nature of the liberty extended to
them, they were instinctively shy of it and
of each other, she chid them gaily for not
availing themselves of their privileges, as if
they abstained from them entirely on her
account.

'You two'—she had got to coupling them
together continually—'are a great deal too
considerate. It ain't in me to be a kill-joy,
but you make me ashamed, though I must
confess that it is a failing I am not given
to indulging in. Why should you not have
your good time as well as others? Don't let
me interfere with you.'

Lady Fermor had naturally her special
seat in her own window of the drawing-room,
and she took to barricading herself in it with
screens, cushions, foot-stools, and little tables
for her various refreshments—biscuits, fruits,
wine, tea, as her habits and the hour required.
She had always been sufficient for herself,
but she appeared to be becoming impatient,
even of the company of a young man of her

own choosing, and to be contracting a passion for solitude.

'You can keep to your own window. You must have a great deal to talk about—young couples always have. Old people have done with everything save thinking, and that, too, goes, I suppose, so that there is only sensation left, poor creatures that we are! But say your say while you have it to do, and want to be out with it; never mind me, I shan't hear a syllable at this distance.'

While the party had been travelling, Lady Fermor had resigned the head of the table to one of her grand-daughters, but she had left the foot vacant. Now she elected that Sir William should play the host opposite Iris as the hostess. And Lady Fermor told them to their faces, in the most innocent manner possible, so that they felt themselves behaving foolishly to blush, that they became their relative positions and discharged their respective duties admirably.

Iris did her best to supply Soames's place in the maid's temporary absence, and was often alone with her grandmother in her bedroom. On these occasions Lady Fermor was even ostentatious in professing her entire satisfaction with Iris's efforts to serve her, which grew bungling, from sheer astonishment and trepidation at the gracious forbearance with which the girl's worst blunders were borne, and the praise indiscriminately awarded to the whole performance.

'I am very much obliged to you, child, you are too attentive; but I ought not to keep you from other duties.'

'Grandmamma, you are laughing at me,' cried Iris in desperation. 'What duties have I in comparison with the obligation to wait upon you, if you will let me? I know I do it very badly, but I hope to improve, and become a proficient abigail by the time Soames comes back.'

'You undervalue yourself far too much. It is a bad practice, which you must not let grow upon you, else people will be sure to take advantage of it. There are plenty of forward, encroaching persons to be met with everywhere; more than that, excessive humility, which is often affectation, does not suit your station in life. You ought to remember your catechism about "the station to which you are called," and think of what you owe to others besides indulging your own inclina-

tions. There now,' said Lady Fermor, after
Iris had enveloped her grandmother in her
dressing-gown and removed her wig, re-
placing it by one of the exploded nightcaps,
which are only in vogue to shelter the bald
pates of octogenarians, 'go down and entertain William.'

Lately Lady Fermor had taken to dropping
the 'Thwaite' and the 'Sir' before the
Christian name, in speaking apart with Iris
of the Squire of Whitehills. The new habit
smote upon Iris's ears with a peculiarly
familiar home-like effect; when the name
was coupled with a dogmatic recommendation
to 'entertain' its bearer, Iris's breath was
taken away. She was not even fit to meet
the cool command with the calm assurance
that Sir William could entertain himself; if
not, he must be the sufferer; she was not
bound to step in to his rescue. She did not
say it, but she failed to return to the drawing-
room; she retired to her own room, and put
her hands before her face.

At the same time neither Iris nor Sir
William could resent mere insinuations,
which after all might owe the most of their
significance to what might have become

their morbid self-consciousness, and troubled
fancies. She knew as well as if she had
heard it what would have been her grandmother's answer if she, Iris, had protested
against the inference cunningly drawn. Lady
Fermor would have cried in the height of incredulous astonishment, 'Child, what did I
say? What could you think was my meaning?' and an explanation of what Iris might
have thought, as it appeared unjustifiably re-
viving all the horrible mischief that had been
set at rest, was too dreadful for a delicate-
minded girl to face without the utmost necessity for the encounter.

Iris seriously revolved the alarming doubt
if her grandmother's mind were giving way
at last, when one day, on two occasions, both
when the ladies were sitting by themselves,
and when Sir William was with them, Lady
Fermor did what she had once done before
on paper, addressed Iris as 'Lady Thwaite.'
'What is your opinion of the weather, Lady
Thwaite?' 'Lady Thwaite, have you seen
the birds in Sir William's bag?'

Iris did not answer. She reserved what
meteorological opinion she had, and whether
she had enjoyed the spectacle referred to,

she only looked down with startled dismay
and shifting colour. She could not have
raised her eyes to meet Sir William's for the
world.

The incorrectly applied title might have
proceeded from a lapse of memory in an old
woman, though Lady Fermor hitherto had
not been liable to such lapses. Anyhow she
did not show that she had observed her mistake by calling herself back or apologising
for it. Her sole comment on Iris's dead
silence on both occasions was by repeating
her inquiries with a little impatience, without
again naming the person spoken to. 'Did
you hear me? What is your opinion of the
weather?' 'Have you seen Sir William's
grouse?'

If the misapplication of the name were
not a slip of the tongue, if taking them along
with other indications they formed an index
that Lady Fermor's once acute and powerful
though neither fine nor cultivated intellect,
and clear steady brains were, as she had predicted, losing their edge, becoming clouded
over, even reeling on their throne, the shape
the disorder of her faculties had taken would
not be at all wonderful. It would be almost

natural that the first of a throng of coming delusions should point to her conviction of the accomplishment of a scheme on which she had so set her imperious will that one of her last rational acts—if it could be called rational—had been to seek to establish an unpardonable fraud by coercing the victims to submit to it, and ratify it, out of shame and terror for a woman's good name.

But what could Iris do in the case? She was left for a week alone, save for Sir William Thwaite, with her grandmother, far from home—viewing distance in the light of Lady Fermor's age and infirmities, in a little Scotch town, which was almost like a foreign watering-place to a girl so little travelled in these travelling days.

It was a new vague danger to be dreaded, along with the constant miserable embarrassment to be endured.

Iris could hardly say how much Sir William Thwaite was struck or what he felt. It was impossible to consult him on the point. Once he had betrayed every emotion of his soul in his face as in a mirror. Further experience of life had taught him to wear a mask to some extent; but in the course of the last few days the mask had fallen occasionally, though only with the effect of electrifying and baffling the beholder more completely. For the shifting expression was, after all, more perplexing than any steadiness of impenetrability. Was Iris, as well as her grandmother, losing her senses, when the girl asked herself which was Sir William's true look, and which exhibited his real state of mind — the bluff impassiveness which he generally kept up, or the glimpses of passion checked in its display, yet with tokens of such profoundness as belonged to the depths of the man's nature ?

The very material world around Iris ; the old-fashioned inn to which Thomas Cochrane and his young wife had come after their runaway marriage ; the braes over which the old moss-troopers had sped in many a moonlight foray, which had sometimes included a disconsolate bride snatched along with her living dowry of lowing kine and bleating sheep from the English side of the border ; the holiday watering-place among the hills, with the holiday company in which were various specimens of lovers, and no lack of newly-wedded pairs come to spend their simple honeymoons—all began to assume an unreal, sympathetic, or mocking aspect to Iris. The strain was becoming too hard for her. She said to herself, with despairing deliberation, she could not bear it much longer. Her grandmother, if she had been in her right mind, had been very wicked to bring such trouble upon two people who had never wronged her, one of whom was her own flesh and blood. She, Iris, must do what she could to prevent the leaven working till it had leavened the whole lump of her own life and that of another ; so soon as Soames returned, the girl would go away as she had gone before, to return no more to Lady Fermor or to Lambford. King Lud would be gone, and Marianne Dugdale ought to come back for a time—it was but right for her to pay her small part of the penalty—or one of Iris's remaining cousins might take her place.

She would tell no one of her departure this time. She had said to Lady Fermor she would not, and her grandmother had forfeited every right to Iris's confidence. She would be less willing than ever to compromise the Actons together with Marianne Dugdale ; and to imply that any other person had a right to the knowledge of what Iris was going to do, would be virtually to lend her countenance to the nebulous tie to which she was eager to put an end. She was to be a runaway twice over, but never a runaway bride. She felt she would rather die than tempt Sir William Thwaite to believe she had been willing to appropriate her share of the *rôle* which had been imposed upon them both. She would go to Mrs. Haigh, and if she could not receive her, she might find a place for Iris, safe, however humble. She would work her fingers to the bone and her eyes till they were blind in their sockets, to maintain herself in honest, honourable independence ; beyond that nothing signified.

The haggard, hunted, scared look was stealing into Iris Compton's little face again, and, glancing into her mirror, she knew she looked old for her years. In addition, she felt she was old—old to indifference and hopelessness for this life, though not for the life to come, and that was her one great ground for thankfulness, which kept her heart from breaking. Iris could not realise that the youth was only beaten down, not trampled out of her, that it was possible for it to

revive and blossom like the rose, that ten
years hence she might be counting herself
still a young woman having a bountiful future
before her, with a grateful, cheerful heart.

Iris's purpose was deferred by Soames's
protracted absence. Lady Fermor did not
grudge it; in fact she was at the bottom
of the delay. She had caused a journey
which might have been accomplished in less
than twenty-four hours, to be broken by a
halt of half as many days. She was length-
ening the halt by keeping Soames at Lambford executing commission after commission
for her mistress at Knotley, Birkett, and
Cavesham, commissions sent to Soames at
the rate of half-a-dozen fresh orders every
morning. Iris did not believe it was Soames's
fault that these could not be executed with
the rapidity of a flash of lightning. The girl
gave the woman credit for fretting over the
length of her holiday. The all-powerful
attraction of the annuity must be drawing
the waiting-maid back, with all that robust
strength of self-interest which has been
allowed to grow without restraint for many a
year. But Iris could wait—all the more
easily in the end, that Sir William had gone

away on an unexplained errand which was to
last a day, but detained him for a couple of
days. Lady Fermor extended her afternoon
drive on both days so that she might finish by
taking the station on her way home and there
awaiting her friend's return. Iris told herself
that she wished he might not return at all
during her stay at Moffat, and she thought
the wish must have looked out at him
from her eyes when he did appear, and Lady
Fermor was calling to him—careless who
might hear her, that he was a naughty man
to put her to the trouble of bringing ¡Iris
twice to the station to fetch him back to the
inn. For after he had driven home with
them, assisted Lady Fermor to alight, and
handed her over to the landlady and her sub-
ordinates, he detained Iris for a moment
behind her grandmother, to say, with an
undercurrent of vexation and reproach in his
voice, ' I will go abroad and stay there, Miss
Compton, if you wish it—you need fear no
annoyance from me ; you have but to say the
word ; I should be gone already, were it not
that you are alone with Lady Fermor.'

That was her own motive for delay, she reflected with an undefined, unreasonable sense

of bitterness. Well, perhaps it was better they should understand each other thoroughly. But she only said—gently, as she imagined, with a chilling rejection of any privilege of standing by her, as he thought, but in truth she hardly knew what she said :

'Don't let any consideration with regard to grandmamma or me interfere with your arrangements, Sir William ; we shall do very well. You can see we have managed perfectly for ourselves during these two days ; besides Soames will turn up presently.'

CHAPTER XLI.

THE mail from the south had come in and
Iris had left Sir William reading the newspapers to her grandmother and gone out for
a solitary walk. She wanted to walk far and
fast till she was wholesomely tired from bodily
fatigue, to be braced by the strong north
country air, and to have the moorland wind
blow away the cobwebs which had lodged
in her brain, were stifling her common-sense,
and torturing her nerves. She had climbed
the hill Marianne had spoken of—one of
those hills which, so far as general resemblance and a name in common go, are
appendages to various towns in Scotland,
being memorials of the last gruesome scene
of all which followed the exercise of the juris-
diction of a baron's court.

The hill was fair to see in its autumn

garniture, and retained no brand of gallows and hangings. It was the object of one of the favourite walks of the place. Marianne had climbed it, but with King Lud in place of Iris for her companion, in a spirit of faithlessness which other maidens have shown before her, and will show to the end of time. Indeed, according to the law of natural selection, such hills are an approved resort for persons in the particular relation which seemed to flourish abundantly, at least in Iris's distempered eyes, at the little watering place.

Perhaps the old naval hero and his runaway bride had climbed the tolerably steep ascent with nimble feet in their day. If so his glorious deeds and the fame which has survived and blotted out his shame might have formed a fitting topic for the other captain bold—save for King Lud's inveterate modesty—to enlarge upon to his mistress, just as the sea king's escapade on shore, with its grievous consequences, haunted Iris with threats and forebodings. Had that old-world couple, with a certain vigorous stamp lingering about their very shadowiness, played their own game in perfect earnest ; or had they, too, been somehow decoyed and forced among quicksands ?

Iris did not anticipate much seclusion in her walk, for the hill was not only frequented by visitors in the season, it was haunted from late spring to late autumn, as she could guess, by children seeking in succession birds' nests, blaeberries, and blackberries; still she could find a quiet spot where she might sit down and rest and look at the wide, free view of hill and hollow and river, just broken here and there by patches of yellow corn-land, stretches of green pasture grass, bits of wood. She could realise that she was in a pastoral country where, whatever human discord broke the stillness, there was always a harmonious undertone made up of the bleating of sheep and the humming of bees among the heather, the occasional bark of a shepherd's dog, the constant trickle far and near of innumerable threads of water which rose and were fed among the hills, to feed in turn the bigger burns and the rivers rushing on to the sea. Overhead was the solemn grey sky of the north country, in which, though there was no sign of rain, the blue was not left long uninvaded, and the white of the fleecy clouds

58—2

was brushed with a silvery grey, passing here and there to deeper, darker, though still clear tints of slate colour.

Iris would fain have let the simplicity and peace of the landscape sink into her harassed mind from which a fantastic nightmare could not be driven out. But she was not left alone to reason with herself, reassure and calm herself by recovering mental balance and spiritual faith, for almost the first thing she saw was Sir William's glengarry rising above the bracken as he pushed his way regardless of the obstacles on a wrong track, to reach her. She was not safe even on the hill of ancient hangings; she was pursued, and caught at that distance from the inn. In despair, she sat quite still and let him come up and speak to her.

'I beg your pardon for intruding upon you, Miss Compton,' he said humbly enough, panting a little from his reckless exertions to gain her side. 'But I have something to say which I am taking the first opportunity to tell you by yourself. It is what you ought to know at once; I have no doubt you will be glad to hear it.'

Iris turned upon him a questioning, apprehensive, half-indignant glance. Then she bethought herself that he was not knowingly to blame for all the misery he had caused, that he was himself involved in the last misfortune. A rush of remorse amounting to tender friendliness came over her for the manner in which she was beginning to treat him, so that she spoke to him quite kindly.

'In place of requiring you to apologise for interrupting my important meditations,' she said, with rather a forlorn attempt at gaiety, 'I ought to thank you heartily, Sir William, for taking so much trouble about something in which you think I have an interest,' and she made room for him to sit down by her.

He threw himself down where she indicated, and was silent for a moment, plucking the heather and looking, not at her, but straight before him with a far-away expression in his eyes. Perhaps he felt what he had already experienced more than once during this year, he was realising the literal circumstances of a bygone dream, in which, however, all the premises had undergone a variation. Not least of all, though that was not in his count, his personal appearance and

general air were changed since Iris had first
known him.   His manliness was more
matured, much that had sat constrainedly
and uneasily on him he now carried lightly
and unthinkingly. He had the look of a
plain, brusque, but not undignified country
gentleman of the class into which his first
sanguine backers had argued he would merge.
The chestnut beard which he wore covered
the somewhat dogged squareness of the jaw
and the weakness of the chin, while the lines
from the nose to the corners of the mouth
were so defined as to give the leonine cast to
the face.   The fulness of forehead beneath
the waves of hair had already a furrow or
two, and the slight contraction of the brow
seemed to set the blue eyes more deeply,
and to cast a shadow over them.   The face
was still massive, tending to ruggedness as it
grew older, with more of thoughtfulness and
of calm repression and patient pain at the
present moment than of its old stern tension
or passionate impulse.

To Iris's surprise, Sir William drew out
his pocket - book and unfolded a written
paper.

' I must first tell you where I have been,

Miss Compton,' he said, and his colour deepened like a girl's while he spoke. ' I've been back to ——,' and he mentioned the inn at which the party had made their last momentous halt.

She would have said :

' What took you there ?' but her lips would not utter the words.

He went on hurriedly :

' I wished to see the landlord, who, so far from seeming a regular blackguard, appeared a respectable enough man. My object was to seek an explanation from him—if an explanation were needed—to ascertain what he had to say of the farce which Lady Fermor insists on keeping up.'

' I dare say you were right,' Iris forced herself to say, half inaudibly, with her eyes turned away, and falling by chance on the little bare hand without the bridegroom's gift of a ring lying languidly on her gown.

' I did not see him at first. By a curious coincidence Lady Fermor had written for him to come here ; but he had to attend some sale. I waited for his return and had a conversation with him. He told me the whole truth, and I made him write it down, and have it witnessed. I took a copy for Lady Fermor, and gave it to her within the last half-hour. This is for you ; all you have to do is to keep it, and it will save you from further anxiety and vexation.'

Iris took the sheet of ruled blue paper in bewilderment. The writing was the round clerkly hand of the best old Scotch parish schools. The diction was not so unexceptionable ; but though the intelligence it conveyed threw a new light on everything, the style ought not to have been incomprehensible, if it had not been for the circumstance that the letters and the sense of the words danced before Iris's eyes and understanding. She could not take them in for some moments. It was only by a supreme effort at self-control that she at last mastered the contents of the paper.

'This is to certify that my house of entertainment at ——, being built on the very boundary-line between the two countries—as there are plenty of records to prove what the "Marches" are—some of its rooms are in England and some in Scotland. The sitting-rooms which were lately occupied by Lady Fermor

and party are both in England. No marriage
ceremony performed according to Scotch law
within the bounds of either of them would be
legal, or could stand. This would be the case
even though the contract had been entered
into in good faith, with the full knowledge
and concurrence of all concerned—whereas
I am assured by Sir William Thwaite, who
acted as the bridegroom in a performance of
which I got a glimpse, that the whole thing
was a mere play or frolic, never intended by
the principal persons engaged in it to go any
farther.

'I wish to say for myself that I believe
the fact of part of the house being in England
and part in Scotland did not exist without
abuse lang syne. Sometimes, to extort
rewards and bribes, the couples who had
whiles betrayed others were themselves betrayed, and were handed over unwed, when
they had thought otherwise, to the friends at
their heels. Or, what was baser still, bride
and bridegroom had to cower their whole life
lang before the auld innkeepers and the mock
ministers, and pay sweetly for their silence on
what, in point of law, was no better than a
mock marriage. Or, if the bridegroom were

a villain, he could cast off his bride through the villainy of his helpers.

'I had no suspicion of what was going on the other night till I was warned by one of the servant lasses, who mistook jest for earnest. I came up, as fast as my feet would carry me, to shift the party into the opposite room, which had first to be cleared of its company. By the time that had been done the business was all but finished, while it looked to me more like a foolish joke than a serious weddin'. In that case, with no harm intended or done, I appeal to any innkeeper in his senses if it was for me to come forward and affront and displease titled customers. If I had got any proof that the marriage was really meant for a wedding which was to be carried out, I hereby solemnly declare that I would have come forward and telled the truth at any cost.

'I admit when the old leddy started at break-òf-day, leaving the couple behind, I misdoubted the joke and tried to get speech of her, but she would not hear me. Maybe she has minded that though, and so has sent for me to go all the way to Moffat to speak with her. And when the gentleman that stood for the bridegroom, who has now come back to clear up the story, left next, that same morning, I thought like the lave that he would be back again in no time, and that it would be soon enough then to warn him. It was rather a ticklish thing, if so be he thought he was wad, to tell him he was mistaken, and bear the wyte of the English rooms which belonged to the building of the house on the very Border a good wheen years before I was born.

' I meant also to speak to the young leddy, though she had sustained no wrong that I know of, but before I had word of her intended departure she too had gone off with a friend that was sent back for her just at the moment when I was engaged with some pressing customers ; and I could not think she would suffer harm in her friend's hands. However, the affair has been on my mind, and I have not been without fear that, jest or earnest, me, and more than me, might get into trouble about it yet. And I was on the eve of travelling as far as Moffat at my own ill-convenience to obey the auld leddy's orders and make a clean breast of it to her, when the gentleman calling himself Sir William

Thwaite, who is, according to his own account, biding at the same inn in Moffat, came
express to me, and saved me the journey.
He has caused me to write this paper, which
he is to show the leddies. He'll certify
that I have been ready to answer all his
questions and to communicate to him the
local disqualification, which attests beyond
dispute that no legal marriage was, or could
have been, celebrated in the front or in the
back-parlour on the second floor of my house
of —— on the evening of the 7th of August,
187—.

'(Signed) ANDREW PEEBLES.

'(Witnessed) JAMES MUSGRAVE.

'CATHARINE PRESTON.'

Iris was free ; no further glamour could be
thrown over an idle incident—an accident,
and the finger of scandal would never point
to her, even in her grave. But the result was
something altogether different from what she
had been brought to dread, and the man who
had freed her, who thus voluntarily renounced
the far-fetched ghost of a claim to her, was
the same who in the hay-field at Whitehills
had persisted against every remonstrance in

declaring his desperate love for her, and
maintained it was no light fancy, but a lifelong passion and sorrow. This was the man
who dissolved the masquerade that yet seemed
to bind them strangely together. But while it
somehow smote her to the heart that he could
do it, she cried out against herself for her
disloyalty to herself and him, and told herself the truth, that if he had acted otherwise he must have degraded himself in her
eyes, and she would have had the double
anguish of learning to despise him at this
date. She must not let him see what she
thought ; she must give him his due. She
turned to him with her hands clasped tightly,
and brilliant roses in the cheeks that were
growing thin.

'How shall I ever thank you, Sir William?
If you had failed me and made me suffer for
a piece of folly, what would have become of
me, and of you also ? But you behaved like
the perfect gentleman and true friend that I
have long known you to be.'

'Come,' he said, catching his breath and
speaking with something of the old rough-
ness, 'don't make it too hard for a fellow.
But I must speak out just this once, since

we shall never allude to the subject again.'

'You might have paid me back for what must have struck you as a girl's intolerable arrogance,' she said, half under her breath.

'No, no,' he corrected her quickly; 'you are talking nonsense now. You could never be arrogant. It was I who was a presumptuous, deluded idiot.'

'You have shielded and delivered me,' she said sadly, 'while I—I believe I have done nothing save injure you since the first time we met.'

'How can you say so?' he cried, impatiently—almost indignantly. 'You made a man of me—by causing me to look up to what was far above my reach certainly—but when I fell back into the beast again have you forgotten how you came and saved both me and poor Honor?'

'Poor Honor!' echoed Iris, and the tears began to trickle down her cheeks in spite of herself, for she had been much tried lately, and the strain on her was, as she had said, becoming more than she could bear.

'Don't cry, Miss Compton, for mercy's sake,' he implored. 'I could not stand it. I could not answer for myself, though at my worst I would not have taken advantage of you in the way you seem to think I might have done. To make out, after one mad moment, that you had married me truly according to the Scotch law, or any law, and to call Lady Fermor to bear me out in the assertion, would have been to act like a rascal as well as a brute, to have lost your friendship, and I have been proud to possess that at least.'

'And now we shall be friends always,' she said wistfully.

'I don't know,' he answered restlessly. 'Yes, friends in heart I hope, if you will do me the honour. But it ain't as if I were another woman or a better man. I think I shall go abroad as I proposed.'

'All the same you will come back to Whitehills one day,' she ventured with a faint smile.

'What, to find you——' he began vehemently, then stopped for an instant, and went on more quietly. 'If I cared for you as you deserve to be cared for, I should not regret finding you in a happier and safer home than where I first saw you, and shall always remember you, at Lambford. But I am a selfish dog.'

She was silent now, breathing with soft quickness.

' I need not say Lady Fermor, though she has tried to be my friend,' he remarked with rather a grim smile, ' is no protector for you, any more than she was for your cousin, Miss Dugdale. But you are another sort of girl— so much wiser and stronger in your gentleness, that it was only after repeated proofs I could think your grandmother might be too much for you. It is exactly as I said the other night at the station ; forgive me for the liberty, but I cannot, as I am a man, endure to leave you with her.'

She continued dumb. She did not say, as she had implied before, that whatever risk she ran it could be nothing to him, or that she resented pity from him ; she did not upbraid him with hurting her by reminding her of her friendlessness ; she did not bid him go again.

He looked at her with the keenest, most earnest scrutiny, flushing high while he looked.

' I am sure you would not trifle with me, Miss Compton. You did not do it before,

when I was a foolhardy ass. Perhaps you
think it is impossible one man can twice err
in the same indefensible way. You know I
was such a blockhead as not to see through
your cousin's merry fencing, and guess on
which side her deliverance lay. I was tempted
to feel that, if she would let me, I ought to
come to the rescue, and not see her sacrificed
as I had seen another bright, kind woman
perish. It seemed all that was left for me
to do. It was not giving up much, for I
had not a grain of hope besides. But I
could not venture to approach you, and
propose to be your protector, not even after
what has come and gone—you are too far
above me.'

She made a hasty deprecating movement
to interrupt him, but he did not heed it.

' And it would be too great a mockery—I
may as well say it, since I am in for it, though
I may affront you again. You have said
enough to show you will not mistake me—I
love you as I love my life. I have done so
from the first moment I saw you ; I shall do
it to my last gasp, though you mayn't like it.
I can't help it any more than you can. And
I might have been content with your toler-

ance—like a scrap thrown to a dog—in the
past; but though I've been down in the
depths since then, things are different somehow with me. I could not be satisfied to-day
with what I should perhaps have caught at
years ago.   I am wiser, or I am prouder,
though I have little enough to be proud of.
I should not ask much, but I must have a
grain—a living seed fit to sprout and grow.
I know only too well what I have been, and
how unworthy I am still; but if you could
ever look over it, like the generous, gentle
soul you are and were to poor Honor—I
don't mind though it were a bit for her sake
—you had a soft heart to her, bless you!
because she has left me alone in the world—
why then I should be the proudest, gladdest
fellow on earth.   I would keep you, as far as
my life could save you, from care and sorrow.
I would serve you with my best, and ask
only a crumb of kindness, and that you yourself should be happy.

She spoke at last. 'Not for Honor's sake,'
she faltered, 'though I did care for her, but
for your own—not a crumb, but all.   Has it
not been well won?' She laid her hand
in his as she spoke, and her pure lips

were there for his reverent awed lips to press, her sweet eyes to return shyly his blissful glances.

After the two had talked long together, Sir William suddenly announced, with a laugh which spoke volumes for the terms to which they had attained : ' I have forgotten to tell you that Lady Fermor was so put out by the paper I brought her, she said she would set off for Lambford to-morrow ; she would not wait for Soames.'

'Well, if grandmamma does it won't matter—will it ? She did not forbid you to accompany her, I hope. I shall be very glad to see home again, to see them all at the Rectory, and hear what they will say. Perhaps we may be in time to catch up King Lud, before he sails. Poor, dear Marianne ! I am sorry for her now.'

' Why in the world should you be sorry ?'

' Because you are not going to sail, Sir William—ought I to tell you that ?'

'If it does not hurt you to say it, it is very agreeable for me to hear it.'

' But it will spoil you, and as it was only the other day that I refused to entertain you, I think you may have some notion how far I was from contemplating spoiling you then. We must not get on quite so fast. But I will say this, that I doubt if King Lud and Marianne are quite so happy as we are.'

'I doubt it too, though I have only one reason to give for the doubt.'

'I don't wish to hear that reason again to-day; I think I have heard it already. I mean because they have not been tried.'

'Perhaps he would not agree with you, poor chap.'

'Oh! but that was all a man's stupidity not to see through her flattering opposition. They have come together without one real tribulation to test them. They strike me at this moment as two quite inexperienced, light-hearted young persons, so that one fears— though one hopes not—that the cares and trials may all lie before them. Now we, though doubtless we have troubles by the score in store for us, have passed through fire and water; we know and can trust ourselves and each other.'

There was trouble in his eyes at that very minute. 'Trusted and tried, and never found wanting—I can say that of you, my sweetheart; but can you ever trust me?'

' Yes, William,' she said with simple sincerity, and so earnestly that there was a little solemnity in her tones ; ' with all my heart. You have fought a good fight, and He who strengthened you for the battle will never suffer you to be vanquished. I shall be glad to be home again,' she added more lightly. ' I have been very unhappy there sometimes, but I feel as if that were all to be forgotten now, and only the peaceful, happy days to be remembered. I was never so long away from home before. Now that I have time to think of it, I want very much to see what changes have taken place in my corner of Eastham during my absence.'

' And you want to see Whitehills again, for Lambford cannot long be your home ; you will begin to look on Whitehills very differently. We may go abroad and see the world, but we must settle at Whitehills ; that will always be the most important place to us.'

' You cannot tell how long ago I was told to give my most serious consideration to Whitehills. Your cousin, Lady Thwaite, will think I have taken her advice,'

' Never mind what she thinks. I suppose she will be pleased, and she will forgive me.

Well, she has forgiven me long ago. But I shall take to her now, for I cannot forget that it was by her means I saw my lady first.'

'It was after that meeting I called you "a good sort of young man" to grandmamma.'

'I am afraid I did not deserve the character. But, Iris, Lady Thwaite is the only pretence to a friend I can give you.'

'And how many can I give you?' she said with an answering sigh.

'I think if you had known my sister Jen you would have loved her, though she had to work to earn bread for her and me, and was a washerwoman to the last day that I left her in peace.'

'I am sure I should,' said Iris, with conviction. 'Nobody, not you yourself, could have been so much obliged to her, and we should have had one chief source of interest in common.'

'There is a good fellow who has been, next to you, since I lost Jen, the best friend I had in the world, though he would never call himself anything save my servant. He will be as proud as a peacock, as pleased as a pike-staff to hear the great news.'

'I know,' said Iris, with a bright smile;

'Bill Rogers. Tell him from me to wish us both joy. His sister has sometimes said that if I had ever a house of my own she would like to go with me. She may if grandmamma consents, mayn't she? Why, we have loads of faithful friends, William.'

When the couple returned to the inn, they had tarried so long that Lady Fermor, in great dudgeon from another cause, had eaten her luncheon without them, and set out on her afternoon drive alone.

Sir William and Iris strolled into the inn-garden. She found an old-fashioned rosebush still covered with roses, the same as some she had seen at the last halting-place. A few hours ago she would have tried not to see those roses; she would not have spoken of them—least of all to Sir William Thwaite; she would have wished to forget that they were there. But a single morning had brought such a change to the depressing, distracting conditions of her life, that she hailed the flowers. She caused him to gather clusters of them, shared them with him, put some of them as before in her jacket. 'Do you remember ever seeing such roses?' she asked him mischievously.

'You are out if you expect to find my memory in fault here,' he told her. 'It ain't the best of memories, but there are some things I don't forget. I could show you the marrow of these in my pocket-book.'

'Then keep them carefully, for they were my single ornament at the rehearsal of the greatest event in our lives.'

The girl was laughing and jesting already, girl-like, at the nightmare of the last two or three weeks. And he was a proud and happy man to note the change in her—proud and happy to have her speaking to him in this fashion.

The whole party dined that day for the first time, by Lady Fermor's choice, at the *table d'hôte* of the inn. There were some inquisitive people present who had seen the titles of two of the party in the visitors' book, and were attracted by the aristocratic old mummy who asserted her importance, and the handsome young couple under her charge. The girl had a head like a cherub, and her companion looked a comely young fellow in the heyday of his life. Clusters of the same rose were in her fichu and in his buttonhole; and the eyes of the wearers had a trick of straying to each other, even in an august presence. It was remarked if my Lady Fermor did not approve of that match, she had brought the pair into a dangerous neighbourhood.

The truth was that at the close of Iris's grandmother's afternoon nap, she had heard of the accomplishment of the marriage, for which she had so long planned, schemed, and striven by fair means and foul, of which that very morning she had received cause to despair. She had got her will; but the question was how far it had lost its charm and become embittered to her by the circumstance that her instrumentality had little or nothing to do with the attainment of her end. She had even been foiled in her last daring, heartless, shameless move; and it was only by their own choice, which they might have exerted any day, that Sir William and Iris were about to marry. Lady Fermor had heard Sir William with little snorts and something not far from a scowl. She had said: 'You have plenty of cheek, Thwaite, to come to me with such a proposal, after the paper you showed me this morning. You two have taken your own time and mode to make up your minds, and have been rather long about it. What if I decide to have my objections now; to say I am sick—which is a fact—of the tiresome affair, and to forbid the alliance to go any further?'

'I am afraid that it is too late, Lady Fermor, after the encouragement you have given me,' said Sir William, keeping his temper. 'I don't ask anything more from you except your grand-daughter, while I am ready to make any settlement upon her that you please. Excuse me, my lady, but you have not exhibited so deep an interest in her welfare or dealt so fairly by her, as to warrant her—a woman who is of age—in declining to act for herself because you bid her.'

'And I have shown you no kindness— have looked over no slips and stumbles on your part? Of course not. Deny that you owe me anything. That is the way of the world.'

But though Lady Fermor had been as- toundingly ungracious and unreasonable in eyes which might have read her better by this time, she was a woman of the world. She did not dismiss Sir William; she ac- cepted, however grumblingly, his escort back to England; and she proceeded to announce the marriage as if it had been from beginning to end of her making.

Before Iris was far across the Border she sent back a letter to Jeannie, the maid at the inn.

'I have taken your advice, Jeannie—not because a happy accident has enabled your master, with James Musgrove and Catharine Preston, whoever they may be, to testify to my deliverance from an unknown danger, not because I fear any scandal in the future, but because I now know certainly what I just guessed before, that Sir William Thwaite is one of the best of men, and that I shall be one of the happiest of women if I marry him in sober earnest. You must not think that I am out of my senses to write this after what I said to you. To convince you of it I will grant that he is not perfect, any more than his fellow-mortals—that he has had his evil days; but he has been made the conqueror, and I am going to share his conquest. I owe it to your kindness to let you know the happy end of the story; and remember, Jeannie, if I can ever serve you in return, count upon me. I enclose Sir William's address for this purpose.'

Lady Thwaite was profuse and tolerably sincere in her congratulations. 'I am glad you have thought better of it, my love. You are a lucky girl; not everybody gets the opportunity of changing her mind to some purpose. I shall be charmed to have you reigning in my place in dear old Whitehills. We will shut our eyes and forget that there was an infatuated, miserable interregnum, with another dreadful Lady Thwaite, between. He will only think the more of you, if he should ever look back and contrast the two. I speak as a relation of the family, my dear Iris.'

'But you are mistaken, Lady Thwaite,' said Iris, with the old involuntary drawing up of her figure and rearing of her little head; 'neither Sir William nor I will ever forget poor Honor. There can be no invidious comparison or contrast between us two. We were brought up very differently, yet we were friends, in spite of every obstacle, when we were children and girls. Do you know the last thing she did before she left Whitehills was to come across to Lambford to bid me farewell? I am glad to think of it.'

'Oh! Well, just as you like, my dear.

You and Sir William are two very remarkable people—about the most remarkable in my circle; and if it please you to recollect what most persons would prefer to forget, it is only a matter of taste; it does not necessarily signify.'

Marianne Dugdale first stared, then said, a little drily: 'I was led to suppose the *penchant* was all on one side; that is, after I had got the faintest hint of a *penchant*. In short, there have been so many different accounts that, upon my word, one is puzzled which to believe.' Then she added, while she struggled between a frown and a smile, 'So you two will be married long before we shall.' But presently the smile gained the supremacy and grew wondrous sweet, and Marianne cried, 'All right!' and kissed Iris with effusion before the whole company, looking as much affronted the next moment as if King Lud had been the object of the caress.

His congratulations were frank and hearty, the Rector and his wife and all the others were complaisant, but Lucy held back a little.

Lucy had been much exercised lately on

the subject of her brother's engagement.
She had been affectionately impressed by the
prize Marianne Dugdale had won. King
Lud's virtue from childhood, his umblemished
character in every respect, had been the
frequent theme of Lucy's laudations. She
had dwelt with justice on these lustrous
jewels in King Lud's crown, until she felt
truly that for any man to be without them,
or to have tarnished their lustre, was a flaw
indeed. Thus the very girl who had given
in her early adherence to Iris's accepting the
fate assigned to her, and complying with her
grandmother's wishes, now sought anxiously
to hold the willing bride back, and to remon-
strate with her on concluding the contract.
It was another and a much more commendable spirit than that exhibited by the Hollises,
who, when they heard of the marriage, protested it was a thousand pities it had not
happened an age ago, when there was a
much greater and more amusing disparity
between the pair, and when poor Sir William
was always shivering on the verge of putting
out the cloven foot ; as it was, the second
Lady Thwaite, though she was a nice enough
girl, and all that sort of thing, would never be

the gain to the jolliness of the neighbourhood
which the first had promised to be.

'Yes, darling,' said Lucy, hesitating a
good deal, 'it is delightful to have you settled so near us after all. It is very pleasant
to think that you can bring yourself to do
what Lady Fermor has so long wished. She
is your grandmother, your nearest surviving
relative, and she has brought you up besides.
I am sure you know I am the very last person
to speak lightly of such obligations. But oh!
Iris, may they not sometimes be set aside?.
So many things have happened since we
talked of this before. You will not be angry
with me for alluding to Sir William's origin,
which is the same as it ever was, of course,
but then we had not the enlightenment of his
low marriage and of his terrible unsteadiness
for a time. I would not vex you for the
world, Iris, but we are such old friends! Is
it not too great a risk? Are you not frightened?'

'No,' said Iris, without anger, though
with a heightened colour; 'and I am glad
that you have spoken out this once to me,
Lucy, for I know you mean it kindly, and I
can tell you everything. Love casts out fear,

and I love him! I have long loved him.
Would you turn from the creature you loved,
because he had been subject to some
deadly disease, which, in spite of all his
brave desperate struggles to throw it off and
regain perfect health, it was just possible
might return and prostrate him again?
Would you not rather cling to him and help
him to meet the enemy? You know there
can be no defeat in the end, because the very
soul of evil was vanquished long centuries ago;
and I have no thought that there will be a
partial defeat. Oh, Lucy, think what his
trials and disadvantages have been and how
he has risen above them, and then measure
him, if you dare—if you have the heart—with
those who were never really called upon to
bear the burden and heat of the day, never
thrown and trampled in the mire—down in
the place of dragons—or faint with the
deadly weakness of ignorance, evil habits,
and undisciplined passions. I can understand it all, because I have been brought up
in a tainted atmosphere, so close to the blot
on my kindred that only one thing could
have kept me clean. What, am I to sit in
judgment on William Thwaite, who has burst

his bonds and trodden them under foot? Do you think I would not rather run a thousand risks than that they should entangle his very feet again? He is free as any man, but bound or free, love can but live and die for its object.'

And he was made a conqueror. Is it so strange a thing to believe that a man who has been once caught in the toils, may yet again go free, with God's own heaven above him, a loving, faithful woman by his side, and little children clasping his knees?

Iris's screen, with the working out of the great artist's idea of the contest between Arachnë and Minerva, found a place in the Whitehills drawing-room among some relics of poor Honor's finery, tenderly dealt with for her sake. Sir William had an immense admiration for his wife's screen, which the embroideress tried in vain to lower to a reasonable moderation. Rumour darkly whispered the master of Whitehills preferred that comparatively stilted piece of embroidery — begging the great artist's pardon—not only to all the old tapestry, but to one of the glories of the house, the semblance of his ancestress with the toy rake, designed and executed by the king of English portrait-painters. Iris was a little afraid that Sir William venerated her Arachnë and Minerva as one of the art wonders of the world, and that there was no help for it. But a man's extravagant appreciation of his wife's handiwork, even though it may interfere with his æsthetic taste, is surely a fault which leans to virtue's side.

Mrs. Haigh and Ju-ju came and saw the screen in its place of honour, and the former on her return to her boarders exalted Lady Thwaite still more than she had exalted 'the Honourable Miss Compton.'

Marianne Dugdale was a great deal with her cousins, even after she had changed her name, during those first partings from her husband, before she had a settled home with its nursery, when the least gust of wind at might among the old trees in the park sent her down to breakfast next morning with her temper in a particularly rasping condition. Then she would rail at the Admiralty for parting husbands and wives, and not letting her sail with King Lud, when she would have been no trouble ; on the contrary, she would have lent efficient aid in setting every bolt and spar of her Majesty's ship to rights.

Whitehills was a great rendezvous of the Actons, from the Rector with his flowery but honest compliments to the youngest of his offspring. Indeed, the place became established in the records of the neighbourhood as a most pleasant and hospitable country house, in which the dowager Lady Thwaite was fain to claim a vested interest.

Lady Fermor having established her grand-daughter very creditably, behaved as if she had done enough, and concerned herself very little with young Lady Thwaite and her doings. The old woman did not grow fonder of the young one, even after Lady Fermor's infirmities increased until she was forced to admit some of Iris's gentle good offices. But to the last Lady Fermor much preferred the attentions of Sir William, to whom she had long ago been entirely reconciled, and any softening of her stout-hearted looks and cynical words were always for him.

So completely were Iris's bugbears dispersed by the genial influence of a good husband and a happy home, that in walking down the main street of Knotley one day,

60—2

and meeting the wreck of a broken-down old man dragging himself along by the help of a servant's arm and a stick, she crossed over, stopped and inquired kindly for him, listening with commiserating interest to his mumbled complaints.

Her first words when she next saw her husband were :

'I met poor grandmamma's friend whom she used to call "old Pollock," in Knotley to-day, the first time for many months. I don't think he was ever very likeable, but how silly I must have been to feel such a horror of him, and now he looks so wretched, feeble, and friendless, poor man ! William, is there nothing we can do for him ?'

THE END.

BILLING AND SONS, PRINTERS, GUILDFORD.

www.ingramcontent.com/pod-product-compliance
Lightning Source LLC
Chambersburg PA
CBHW031151120726
47905CB00006B/1895

* 9 7 8 3 3 3 7 0 4 8 1 2 9 *